"As unpredictable as an El ̃ ...
and full of electricity as an August Santa Ana wind,
these thirteen wonderfully intriguing stories by
Los Angeles Sisters and Brothers in Crime
will raise your hackles and
cause you to double-lock your doors.
Who said earthquakes and mudslides
were the only terrifying things in Southern California?"

Earlene Fowler
Goose in the Pond

"*Murder by Thirteen* sparkles with intriguing stories
and offers something for every taste
from the gritty to the genteel.
Especially notable are the wackily entertaining
L.A. Justice by Kris Neri
and the superbly plotted
Trickery by Judith Klerman Smith.
This Sisters in Crime anthology is definitely a winner."

Carolyn Hart
Death in Lovers' Lane

"Something for everyone's table,
and some characters I would love to meet again in longer
works, most especially Bea Silver.
I should like to be told when she returns."

Anne Perry
Weighed in the Balance

"...a first-class collection.
The stories are well-wrought, exciting, atmospheric, and
as twisty as the streets of Echo Park.
If you want to understand something about the *real* L.A.,
read these stories."

Rebecca Rothenberg
The Bulrush Murders

"Murder by Thirteen showcases solid work
by a group of new writers that
runs the gamut from the lightest cozies through clever puzzles
to the meanest streets.
One or two are clearly trial runs for potential novel characters.
I especially enjoyed the pieces by Rosalind Roland,
Jinx Beers, Kris Neri and Larry Hill."

Michael Collins
Cadillac Cowboy

"Sisters in Crime/L.A. delivers
a delectable smorgasbord of short mysteries."

Annette Meyers
These Bones Were Made for Dancin'

"The Los Angeles Chapter of Sisters in Crime has
no shortage of talent,
and is to be commended for giving readers
the opportunity to be introduced to some fine writers in
Murder by Thirteen.
Make note of your favorites—
you may be seeing more of their work in the future!"

Jan Burke
Hocus

"Thirteen is a lucky number for readers of these
intriguing, tightly-plotted stories with
memorable characters and fresh voices that
run the gamut from the ironic to
the comical to the mystical and show the
many faces of murder."

Rochelle Majer Krich
Speak No Evil

Murder by Thirteen

Edited by
Priscilla English, Lisa Seidman and Mae Woods

CROWN VALLEY PRESS
Acton, California

Published by Crown Valley Press, P.O. Box 336, Acton, CA 93510-0336.

Cover design by Gayle Partlow, Altadena, CA.
Interior layout and design by Crown Valley Press.

Printed and bound in the United States of America.
First Edition, Second Printing, 1997.

ISBN 0-9647945-3-5

LCCN 97-65292

Contents

Preface

Murder by Thirteen presents thirteen new mystery stories by Los Angeles-based writers. The stories cover a broad terrain—from the barrios to Beverly Hills to the Brontë sisters' crumbling mansion—and differ greatly in tone and style. They do share two common denominators: All deal with murder, and all were written by members of the Los Angeles Chapter of Sisters in Crime. This local organization is part of a national network that has had a profound impact on mystery writing over the past decade.

In 1986, Sisters in Crime was formed by a group of female writers who regularly encountered each other at mystery events and became friends. They shared the concern that mystery writing was considered the domain of tough-talking American men and a few noteworthy English women, an outdated perception being reinforced by newspaper reviews. Statistics verified that reviewers covered fewer mysteries written by women than by men, despite the fact they sold as well, or often better, than new books by men.

Led by Sara Paretsky, the friends became activists. They formed Sisters in Crime to celebrate the work of women in the mystery field and educate the public (reviewers included) about their history and accomplishments. Novelist Marilyn Wallace solidified the mission of the organization when she agreed to edit an anthology of short stories entitled *Sisters in Crime*. The book's success led to four subsequent volumes. The series, now reprinted around the world, has introduced readers to an array of women writers and demonstrated that mystery anthologies continue to have great commercial appeal.

Over the past decade, Sisters in Crime has flourished. This supportive network provides information, helps publicize its authors and encourages new voices. The list of women who have served as president of the national organization is an illustrious "who's who" of the mystery world: Sara Paretsky, Nancy Pickard, Margaret Maron, Susan Dunlap, Carolyn Hart, P.M. Carlson, Linda Grant, Barbara D'Amato, Elaine Raco Chase and Annette Meyers.

The Los Angeles Chapter of Sisters in Crime (SinC/LA) was organized in 1988 by Phyllis Miller, a nonfiction writer and mystery fan. Founding members included authors Wendy Hornsby, Rochelle Krich, Gerry Maddren, Carol Russell Law and Anita Zelman, plus bookseller Terry Baker of Mystery Annex at Small World Books.

In the early days, meetings were held at a local mystery bookstore. An article about the group in the *Los Angeles Times* brought a flock of new members to the tiny shop. People lugged chairs from home, sat on the floor or on top of book tables. The guest speakers were exhilarating. Each month, you could meet and question a real-life female private eye, police officer, lawyer or reporter and, of course, many published mystery writers. No discussion was off-limits: One of L.A.'s coroners gracefully answered questions about how to kill someone and get away with it.

Today, SinC/LA's monthly meetings are held at the South Pasadena Public Library. The chapter continues to recruit provocative and illuminating guest speakers, to share information about writing opportunities and to further the goals of the national organization. It has a diverse membership of women and men, which includes working writers, aspiring writers, teachers, librarians, book dealers, film and TV professionals and mystery fans.

Over the years, SinC/LA has undertaken many ambitious projects. The group hosted a "Guide to Hollywood" half-day presentation featuring television producers and writers at Bouchercon '91. It co-sponsored a special evening with Sara Paretsky at the Writers Guild of America. More recently, SinC/LA inaugurated "No Crime Unpublished," an annual conference for new writers, and published *Desserticide aka Desserts Worth Dying For,* a cook-book that pairs dessert recipes with tongue-in-cheek advice for the would-be murderer.

Continuing in the Sisters in Crime tradition of activism, the chapter has produced this anthology of short stories to exhibit the talents of many of its members. Stories were submitted anonymously and selected on the basis of characterization, originality, mystery plot and narrative voice. Several authors featured in this anthology are in print for the first time. Others are experienced professionals. We believe all are writers you will be reading and enjoying many times in the future.

— Mae Woods

Sisters in Crime
Membership

Membership in Sisters in Crime is open to anyone who has a special interest in mystery writing and in supporting the goals of the organization. Its mission is "to combat discrimination against women in the mystery field, educate publishers and the general public as to inequalities in the treatment of female authors, and to raise the level of awareness of their contribution to the field."

There are currently forty local chapters in the USA, Canada and Europe as well as a GEnie chapter on the Internet. For information about joining Sisters in Crime, please contact:

Sisters in Crime
M. Beth Wasson, Executive Secretary
PO Box 442124
Lawrence, KS 66044-8933
(913) 842-1325
e-mail sistersincrime@juno.com
or
SinC/Los Angeles Chapter
PO Box 251646
Los Angeles, CA 90025
(213) 694-2972

Acknowledgments

Our thanks go to the Anthology Committee and the Board of Directors of SinC/LA, with special acknowledgment to President Kris Neri; Paulette Mouchet, who coordinated and oversaw publication of the book; and Gayle Partlow, who contributed such inspired cover art.

The editors would also like to thank the following people for their help and guidance: Claire Carmichael, Denise Di Pasquale, Charlene Gallagher, Sandy Siegel and Susan Stephenson.

Angels Flight

Paul D. Marks

Dateline: Los Angeles. Echo Park Lake. Peaceful. Serene. Palm trees. Lily pond. Calm. Tranquil. The city dredges the lake every few years. Lotsa junk. Beer bottles. Old tires. Sometimes a rusted iron. Once, a car.

This year, a decomposed body.

Near the lily pond.

Pretty far gone.

Five feet seven inches.

Slight frame.

Narrow hips.

Male? Female?

Examine the body.

If you can call it that.

More like a skeleton.

With a few hempy strands of fetid flesh dangling off.

It was Lucy Railsback's first assignment for the mayor's office. Her first murder. Is this really what four years of college as an economics major had prepared her for? Is this where she expected to be? She had applied for the position in the mayor's office; she wanted to be involved. Never expected to meet a dead body her first day out. She hadn't yet met the LAPD officer she'd been assigned to. From where she stood, on the sidelines, it looked like he wasn't interested in meeting her.

"Gonna be near impossible to figure out who this was," Lucy heard Tom Holland say. He was standing several yards away, near the body. She was by the police ribbon, with the other outsiders. This wasn't how she'd expected it to work.

If this is the nineties, Holland was living in another era. Only in his thirties, he looked like a dinosaur on the new LAPD. His sixties gas-guzzling GTO muscle car and retro fifties pompadour said it all. He was no Alec Baldwin in the style department.

"Nothing's impossible," Jeremy Toler, the assistant coroner, said.

Lucy watched Holland open the skeleton's mouth. She was still several yards away, but the stench drifted toward her. Nobody from ComPAC, the mayor's Community-Police Action Committee, had prepared her for the reality of what she might have to face. The worst stain on their C&R suits and ties was from Philippe's French dip, not from a putrid, decaying body dredged up from the lake. She wasn't sure if she should go down and introduce herself or wait until the lieutenant did the honors. She knew no one would really be honored.

"Not much in the way of teeth," Holland said. "Dental records won't be much help. 'Sides, you're always too damn optimistic."

"It's a sunny L.A. day. What's not to be optimistic about?"

"City's falling apart around you and you're playing *Mr. Rogers' Neighborhood.*"

"Tom." Lieutenant Alvarez's pencil-thin mustache gave him a rakish air. If he were wearing a double-breasted suit with a fedora, he might have stepped out of a forties Bogart movie. Serious eyes betrayed the dashing tone set by the mustache.

"Yeah, boss?"

Alvarez put his arm around Holland's shoulder, walked him away from the edge of the lake, under a palm tree that didn't provide much shade.

"What is it? Can't be good."

"Department's assigning a liaison to you."

"What the…"

"Remember your blood pressure."

"All cops got high blood pressure."

"Several community representatives are being assigned to various dicks and uniformed officers. One's going to spend a few days with you. See how we operate."

"Yeah, and report back to some commission or other about what beasts we are."

"That's out of our hands. Just do your job."

"With a spy looking over my shoulder. How'd I get picked for this gig?"

"It was random. Computer generated."

"Computers'll be the end of me yet."

"Get with the program, man. This is the nineties, almost a new millennium."

"Yeah. I know."

Alvarez pointed to Lucy. Holland saw a woman in her late twenties, early thirties. Hard to tell from his position. She cut a striking slim figure, like an African Lobi shrine. The rainbow-colored African wrap dress heightened the effect. "That's her."

"What ax does she have to grind?"

"I can tell this is gonna be a good one." Alvarez walked Holland toward her. She was standing near the police ribbon, away from the body. At close range, Holland saw her features were sharp, her skin a smooth ebony. Her almond eyes were striking. Exotic.

"Lucy Railsback, Tom Holland."

They shook hands. He looked her straight in the eyes. She stared back at his LAPD blues.

"Holland's the detective in charge of this investigation, Ms. Railsback. You'll be assigned to him, traveling with him. He'll show you the ropes." Alvarez walked off, toward a mob of press.

"What happened here, Detective?"

"Hard to say. City workers found a body when they drained

the lake for cleaning."

Lucy headed toward the body. She knew she had to show Holland she could hack it before he got any wrong ideas about her.

"I wouldn't go over there if I was you."

The skeleton lay blanching in the sun. Lucy leaned over it, pulling a notepad from her purse. Holland stepped behind her, ready to catch her if she fainted. Didn't happen. Instead she spent several minutes curiously looking over the body, scribbling notes. She felt her stomach churning, a miniature tsunami ready to explode. It took all her powers not to turn away, not to let her stomach lose control. She didn't want the detective to see any weakness.

Chagrined, Holland said, "Now you know just about all that I do."

Lucy stepped over the police ribbon, which glinted and twisted in the sun. Watching it gyrate reminded her of her stomach. She moved behind a sturdy date palm, where Holland wouldn't see her.

Holland talked with Toler, the coroner's on-site rep. Holland liked Toler, even though there was always some shred of food hanging in his droopy walrus mustache. Today it looked like pepperoni pizza. Holland could see Lucy on the other side of the ribbon, pacing back and forth. Deep in thought.

"New partner?" the assistant coroner said. Holland looked like he had just swallowed a bad piece of meat at the corner taco stand.

***

"You don't like me hanging around, do you?"

"I didn't say anything." Holland swept a stockpile of greasy fast-food hamburger wrappers and soft drink cups off the seat onto the floorboards. Lucy settled in. He put the GTO in first.

"You didn't have to." Lucy stretched. Shoved the wrappers back under the seat with her feet. Wiped her fingers on a lacy handkerchief she pulled from her purse.

"Don't mind that stuff. Gotta eat on the run most-a the time."
He shifted into second. "Hey, all that grease and oil, it water-proofs the car."

Lucy cracked the slightest smile. The tension in the air was
no longer as thick as the grease on the hamburger wrappers. It
was quiet for a few minutes when Holland broke in:

"I'm a cop. I can't be baby-sitting you while—"

"You aren't baby-sitting me." Lucy thrummed the small spi-ral notebook in her fingers.

"What're you gonna do if things get ugly? If we have to shoot
it out?"

"I'll duck."

He laughed. She smiled.

"Am I really a hindrance to your job?"

"My job is to protect and serve, not coddle political activists."

"I'm one of those you're sworn to 'protect and serve.'"

"What are you doing here?"

"Your new chief, the police commission and the people of
Los Angeles want—"

"That's not what I meant. What are *you* doing here?"

"Just trying to do my duty as a citizen."

"If the citizens would get out of the way and let us cops do our
jobs—"

"Sometimes you do them too well."

"And sometimes—"

"Let's face it, Detective, it's been two days and you've got
nothing."

"I told you the first day it wasn't gonna be easy. Prob'ly dumped
the body in the lake in the middle of the night. And anyone who
might have seen something is too scared to talk."

"Hell, I could solve the case in a flash."

Holland looked at her. *What was this civilian getting at?*
Had she read one too many mystery novels?

"When do they bury the body?" she said.

"Coroner releases it tomorrow. And what the hell are you
talking about?"

"Just bury the body with an eggshell in the palm of each hand."

He looked at her like she was ready for a straitjacket sizing.

"Put eggshells on top of the grave. In a week, maybe less, you'll have your murderer."

There was a slight change in her demeanor, hardly noticeable, except to a detective. Was she serious? Scorn rode Holland's face. Lucy smiled. Holland's eyes left the road, wandering to her. His front bumper jammed up close to the car in front of them.

"Moron," Holland yelled, slamming the brakes. They squealed to a stop. The smell of burnt rubber squeezed out the odor of stale hamburgers.

"Down home in Louisiana there's a story about this fella, Elijah Pantaine." Lucy toyed with the African bracelet on her wrist. "Murdered his girlfriend in a fit of jealous rage and dumped her over the levee. When they found her body, a voodoo priestess placed fresh eggshells in each of her hands and sprinkled some on her grave. Next day, the body of Elijah Pantaine was found floating in the river in just about the same spot where his girlfriend was found."

"And you believe all that?"

"So I guess you won't be wanting my help," Lucy said.

"It's a swell idea. Pass the magic fairy dust."

They drove past Angels Flight, the famous old funicular railway that was recently restored. The old Angels Flight was romantic and practical at the same time. Lucy liked that and said so.

"What a waste of time and money," Holland snorted.

"And what would you have spent it on, bringing another football team to L.A.? A team that might stay all of three years?"

"Crime. More cops. New cars. New computers."

"I believe in that. But sometimes you need something for the soul."

"Will Angels Flight bring back the glamour of the old days? Hollywood's lost its tinsel. Venice's lost its pier. And there are no angels in the City of Angels. What can Angels Flight do to bring that back?"

Holland dropped Lucy off at her house, a small Spanish Colonial Revival in Silverlake, close enough to walk to Echo Park, if you didn't mind running the gang gauntlet. He walked her to the door, hoping she'd invite him in, though he wasn't sure why. She didn't. He got a quick peek inside. Slim, black African statues stood on either side of an entry hall table. The centerpiece of the table was a sleek, shiny black cat statuette with glowing eyes, staring straight at Holland. He shifted to the other side. The eyes shifted with him. Eerie. He said goodbye, hit the road.

Lucy aimlessly wandered around her house. It had been an eye-opening day. This Holland was a hard-head. But she also worried that she was possibly being too hard on him. Of course, if he knew her background, he'd probably demand to have her removed from the case. She sat on the sofa, staring at the shrine, until her eyes could no longer focus and sleep slam-dunked her.

Instead of going home, Holland headed back to Echo Park. Stared at the empty lake. *Dead,* he thought. *Drained of its life. Like L.A.* He remembered when his grandparents used to take him boating here. People still did that, but today they often had to dodge bullets. Not so back then. It was a different city.

He pondered the case. Came up with nothing and headed back to his car. Four young boys passed him on the sidewalk. They were singing a familiar tune, "This Land Is Your Land." But the words were different: "This land is my land, it isn't your land. I've got a shotgun, and you don't got one. I'll blow your head off, if you don't get off. This land is private pro-per-ty."

They couldn't have been more than eight or nine years old.

***

Tick-tock. Tick-tock. The clock on Holland's night stand ticked off time. Every second, another lifetime. Every minute, another eternity. TV droned in the background. Leno. Letterman. Local news. Infomercials. *Dragnet* reruns. Recycled stand-up comedy. He didn't hear a thing.

Stared at his blank walls. No statuettes here. No snarling glow-in-the-dark cats. Nothing. Just empty space.

Negative space.

Phone jangle. Startled. Shaky hand reaching.

"Yeah."

"Holland? Jeremy Toler, coroner's office."

"Don't you guys ever sleep?"

"Thought you'd want to know about your DB."

"Shoot."

"Someone already did. Bullet fragments caught in the flesh, what's left of it. Barely enough to make the gun or do ballistics on, but I'll try. Definite bullet, though."

"Male or female?"

"Female. Don't know the race. Been decomposing about a month, maybe two, I'd say. The water has a high acid content."

"Thanks." Thanks for all the great info. Click. Still nothing to go on. Eyes darting back and forth across the ceiling. Dancing floaters skim across the wall.

Lids closing. Heavy. Sleep is never easy. Never long enough. Never deep enough. Grateful for anything at this point.

Phone jangle.

What time is it? After two.

"Yeah."

"Holland? Detective Tom Holland?"

"Who is this?"

"Stay the hell away from the body in the lake."

"Who the hell is this?"

"Like I'm gonna tell you." Laughter. Click.

***

"And you don't know who called?" Lucy said, getting into Holland's car.

"No. Nondescript voice. Could've been anyone. Male. That's all I know." Holland gulped stale coffee from a thermos. He had filled Lucy in on the coroner's call and on the mysterious call warning him not to pursue the case. "Maybe you can sacrifice some chickens tonight and tell me who did it."

"I'm sorry I brought it up at all." She pulled out her notebook and pencil. "Resistant to new ideas," she said, writing. The writing was more of an intimidation tactic. Holland said what he said in a joking way. Still, it was clear that he wasn't going to accept her on face value. So, she thought, if he was concerned about what report she would make to ComPAC, maybe then he would open up to her. If he knew that she had been trained as a macumba voodoo priestess, he would laugh her off the mayor's committee. She didn't know if she really believed, but her father and mother, who had come from the West Indies in the early sixties did, and they thought she should have "something to fall back on." She hadn't had to use it yet. She doubted she'd use it now. It was more to needle Holland. She enjoyed that.

"You don't believe all that, do you?"

"All that mumbo jumbo. That what you mean?"

He stared at the African charm bracelets on her left hand. Her wrist was narrow and slender. As was the rest of her. She looked like she could have been the model for the statues in her entry hall. "Look, it seems we've gotten off on the wrong foot. Maybe we should start over."

"No wrong feet here. You're just doing your job, I'm doing mine. So, what's on the agenda today?"

"More questioning people around the lake."

"You've done that for three days now. Seems like a dead end. No?"

"Yes, but there're no leads. And with all the publicity about finding a body in the lake, the lieutenant wants me to pursue it. Waste of time as far as I'm concerned."

"I'm sure the woman's family wouldn't consider it so."

"Maybe not. But there're no clues. Nothing. Talking to people till I'm blue in the face isn't gonna change anything. And there's a hell of a lot more cases I could be working on that might actually get me somewhere."

"I understand what you're saying, but—"

"You think I'm not doing my job."

"I think you're doing it as you see fit."

"Thanks." He got out of the GTO, grabbed his windbreaker,

put it on over his shoulder holster. Lucy scrambled behind him.

With the lake drained, the park was nearly empty. The lake looked like a giant mud bath. Holland pulled a small suitcase from the trunk of his car, headed for the bank. Sat down on a bench near where the water would have been if the lake was filled.

"What's in there, forensic equipment?"

"Yeah." He opened the suitcase. Pulled out a pair of mid-calf rubber boots, took his shoes off and put the boots on. He pulled out a large wire-mesh net. "All the best money can buy. Modern equipment."

"I thought the forensic team already went over the lake bed with metal detectors and all kinds of high-tech stuff."

"Can't hurt to double-check. Sometimes the old-fashioned ways are best."

She slow-grinned him. "Like voodoo?"

He ignored her, waded into the mud where the lily pond had been.

"And what am I supposed to do while you're playing mudcakes all day?"

"You're welcome to join me."

The grin slipped from her face. After hanging back for a couple of minutes, Lucy sat on the same bench, kicked off her shoes and removed her pantyhose. She picked her way across the rough ground to the lake bed. Holland looked up.

"What're you doing?"

"Joining you."

"You're crazy. There could be sharp glass, busted cans. You'll hurt yourself."

She pulled the small notepad and pencil from her pocket. "Sexist attitude," she said aloud, while doodling little nothings on the page. He looked at her.

"Thanks."

"Just doing my job, like you're doing yours." She stumbled into a sucking hole. Regained her balance before Holland could muck his way over to help. "I can handle it."

He went back to dredging the lake bottom. Tiring. Exhausting work. Sweat soaked through his shirt, waterlogging the windbreaker, wetting his leather holster. The astringent smell of wet leather filled his nostrils.

"You don't have another one of those for me, do you?" Lucy said, looking at his net. He shook his head. She pawed the mud with her hands, squeezing it through her fingers. "Maybe I'll find something valuable here."

Three bangers in baggy pants and backward Raiders caps roamed the edge of the lake. They eyed the suitcase Holland had left on the bench. One of them turned in his direction. He flashed his badge their way. They flashed gang signs with their fingers, ending with the universal finger sign. Moved on.

After three hours, Holland and Lucy had turned up nothing. They waddled toward the shoreline. With each step, their feet sank into the mire and had to be pulled out by hand. A few feet from dry land, Lucy slipped. Sludge oozed over her face, covering her mouth, eyes and nose. Holland tried to pull her out, was sucked in himself. Both were covered head to toe in the black muck. She finally managed to pull herself up.

"The Creature from the Black Lagoon." She put her hand out to help Holland up.

"And her brother." Laughing, they headed to the bench. "Don't worry," he said, "we'll bill the people of Los Angeles. After all, it was in the line of duty."

"Protecting and serving."

"Right."

"We can shower at my place. It's close."

"What'll I do for clothes?" he said.

Traffic along Sunset moved slowly. Holland kept looking in his rearview mirror.

"What's wrong?"

"I get the feeling we're being followed."

"Who would want to follow us?"

"Bangers maybe."

"In broad daylight?"

"I don't know. Can't tell. There's a yellow car two, three cars back that's been with us almost since we left the park."

"Cop paranoia."

"Maybe."

She led Holland through the arched portico to the back door. A neighbor woman watched.

Tom picked up a hose.

"What're you doing?"

He turned the spigot. A spray of cold water hit Lucy head on. She shivered.

"Don't wanna mess up your house."

"How thoughtful of you."

"This is the *serving* part."

Both of them stripped to their underwear and hosed each other off as best they could, dancing under the stream of water, so it would hit every part of them. Lucy disappeared into the house. Holland waited on the service porch. She returned a moment later with a robe for him. She was already wearing one of red, black and green. He slipped off his underwear. She took his things.

"Now what?" he said.

"I could run them over to the one-hour cleaners. You can shower while I'm gone."

"What about the guy following?"

"Cop paranoia, remember?" Lucy showed Holland where the bathroom was, took his clothes, dressed and headed for the cleaners. The hot shower felt good on his tired muscles. He put the robe back on, waited for her in the living room. A small stone altar sat in the corner. Surrounded by candles. African masks. Charm bags of various sizes. A stuffed boa constrictor, almost twenty feet long, twined around the altar.

When Lucy returned, Holland was lounging on the living room sofa. She handed him his clean clothes.

"Don't you look loose and kicked back, Detective Tom Holland." Lucy's mouth and eyes were pulled tight.

"Maybe, but you sure don't," Holland said, moving behind a decorative Chinese screen. He pulled on his underwear.

"I think you're right. It's getting on my nerves. Your paranoia's catching. I think I was followed."

He shot out from behind the screen, checking at the windows.

"I think I lost him. No one's out there now."

"Can you describe him?"

"Like you said, yellow car. One man in the front seat."

"One of the bangers we saw at the park?"

"I don't think so."

Tom stared at her charm bags. "Maybe you should've taken one of your voodoo amulets with you. Protect you."

She thought he said it almost without joking this time.

"Gris-gris." She pulled a small pouch from under her blouse. "Good luck charm. And, as you can see, no harm came to me."

"You still look worried."

"I can worry all I want, but I trust the charm."

"What's it made of?"

"Bone, goofer dust, graveyard dirt, colored pebbles, salt and ground red pepper."

"I can see how that would keep the evil spirits away." He was joking again. Was she?

***

Gravel crackle.

Look up.

Hearts beating double time.

No time to finish dressing.

Holland grabs Beretta.

Surprised to see Lucy pull out a semi-auto Smith & Wesson.

Safeties off.

Finger triggers.

Check windows.

Check doors.

Nothing.

Ease out back door.

Dusk.

Dark. Gray.

Eyes scanning.

Adjusting to the light.

Click.

Another safety off.

Crack. Three shots fired.

Duck behind patio wall.

Return fire.

Yelp.

Like a wounded animal.

Hit the target.

Footsteps running.

Echoing.

Give chase.

In underwear.

Lucy going for phone.

9-1-1.

Over the fence.

Barefoot.

Through the bush.

Shit.

Nettles.

Dogging through the bush.

Trip.

He's gone.

Damn.

Jam it back to the house.

Cops arriving.

Fill 'em in.

They're off, combing the area.

But the suspect's gone.

"You okay?" Lucy said, looking at Holland's bloodied feet.

"Yeah." He sat on a breakfast-room chair. She brought a washcloth, soap and iodine. "What, no magic potion?"

"Your problem, Tom Holland, is that you don't believe in anything." She worked on his wounds, cleaning, bandaging, with the efficiency of an emergency-room tech.

He had no response. She was right. "Thanks," he said quietly, "for fixing me up."

"Didn't your mama ever tell you not to run outside without shoes?"

He stifled a laugh. Lieutenant Alvarez came in.

"Did you get a look at him?" Alvarez said.

"It was dark. My eyes hadn't adjusted to the light yet. He had dark hair, brown, black, hard to tell."

"We'll find him. You think this is related to the lake?"

"We both thought we were being followed earlier. But no ID on the car."

"I know this is a silly question, but what the hell were you doing out there in your skivvies?"

"He was protecting and serving, Lieutenant," Lucy said with a laugh in her voice. Alvarez looked to Holland.

"Protecting and serving, sir." There was no hint of irony in his voice.

Holland filled in the lieutenant. After an hour of searching and talking to neighbors, the police came up empty-handed, except for a small, fresh bloodstain and expended rounds, some of Holland's 9 mils, the suspect's .32s. But, as the lieutenant had said, unless they had other evidence to compare it to, it was useless. Paramedics checked Holland's feet; couldn't improve on Lucy's work. After the cops left, Holland and Lucy sat in her living room, at opposite ends of the couch. The sun was down, the street dark. Not quiet. Cars whizzed by. Voices shouted in the distance. Music played, a melange of salsa, rock and rap, coming from every direction. Holland longed for sleep.

"What now?" Lucy said.

"Think I'll hit Tommy's for a burger and head home."

"That's not what I meant."

"I don't know. You want a watch put on your house?"

"I'll be all right." Lucy pulled the sixteen-round Smith & Wesson semiautomatic pistol from under a pillow. "They've got a lot of chutzpah coming here."

"They or he, or whoever, doesn't want us nosing around. But hey, they're refilling the lake tomorrow."

"They are?"

Holland nodded.

"Isn't that going to—"

"We won't find anything there. There're no clues. Nothing to go on. I wish the lieutenant would release me from this assignment so I can work on things there's a chance of solving."

"Triaging your cases."

"There's no other way."

A slow smile burned across Lucy's lips. Holland saw. Turned away. When he didn't bite, she said, "There's one other way."

Holland ignored her, said, "If you don't want official LAPD protection, I'm gonna head home."

"If you like, I'll make you dinner. I make a mean omelet."

"With goofer dust?" He smiled, agreeing to stay. It wouldn't sit as heavy as Tommy's. He watched Lucy delicately crack the eggs and mix them. Instead of throwing the shells out, she set them atop the window sill. *Odd,* Holland thought. The omelet was filled with three cheeses, ham, chili peppers.

"Best meal I've had in months," Tom said.

"Probably the only real meal you've had."

They talked for a while. Despite himself, he enjoyed her company. He thought she felt the same. But he couldn't bring himself to take the conversation personal. Too many obstacles still to be overcome. Maybe one day.

He stared at the wall, said, "The worst cases are the unsolved ones. Unsolved murder cases are never closed. But it's not like fiction, where you can always tie things up."

"Do you ever become hardened?" she asked.

"You can't help it some. But you can't grow calluses on your heart."

She walked him to the front door. He couldn't hold the smile back now. Hugged her. Left. Heard the bolt click into place as he headed to his car.

A few minutes later, Lucy sprinted out to her car, got in and drove off.

***

Two nights later.

Holland couldn't stop thinking about Lucy. Maybe she was right about needing something for the soul. Maybe she was right about Angels Flight, too.

Phone jangle.

"Yeah," Holland said. He hadn't gotten a decent night's sleep in a week. Hadn't gotten a good night's sleep since he made detective four years ago.

"Tom, you ain't gonna believe this," Alvarez said on the other end of the line.

An hour later, at 3:03 A.M., Holland, Alvarez, Toler and a gaggle of cops were wading in the shallow water of the lily pond at Echo Park Lake. A shirtless body was floating face up, half in the lake, half out. Dark brown hair lapped at the water's edge. A makeshift bandage covered what appeared to be a bullet wound in the upper left shoulder.

The lieutenant droned on about how, with the shoulder wound, this was probably their guy—the guy Holland had winged at Lucy's. Holland knew it was. That's what scared him. He had no ID. But Holland knew when they matched blood samples, this would be the man who had shot at him two days before. A gun was tucked in his waistband. He knew the shells would match the expended rounds at Lucy's and in the corpse from the lake.

Bulging, petechial eyes said the man had been strangled.

Pristine white eggshells in each of the man's hands said something else.

PAUL D. MARKS is a Los Angeles native who loves the city that L.A. was. Dodging bullets, he's not sure about the city it is today. *Angels Flight* is his first published fiction. He has, however, optioned several of his screenplays to film producers and has had shows produced on PBS and HBO. He is currently at work on a mystery novel.

Everything Is a Matter of Timing

Jinx Beers

The speedometer needle quivered slightly at eighty-seven, then held steady at ninety miles per hour. Jill's hand held firmly on the steering wheel, even though two bright headlights grew larger as they approached in a head-on collision course.

Under Jill's guiding hand and heavy foot, the dusty, cream-colored, souped-up Chevy Impala was in the middle lane of the southbound freeway. But Jill was driving north.

The soft wail of a police siren barely penetrated the windows over the roar of the engine.

The speedometer inched its way up toward one hundred miles per hour. Five hundred feet in front of Jill, the driver of the on-coming car awoke to the fact that some crazy was driving the wrong way on the freeway! He didn't realize he had less than three seconds of closing time at the speeds of the two vehicles. He didn't think about anything, but twisted his steering wheel hard to the right. His lightweight Toyota Celica flipped across the right lane, coming to rest upside down in a bank of pink ice plant along the shoulder of the roadway. Jill, already a half mile away, wasn't aware of what had happened. Not a nerve had twitched.

At three in the morning, especially an early Monday morning, the freeway was nearly deserted. Jill only had to out-guess the movements of the few cars she might encounter. Instinct told her to hold the middle lane and let other cars do the scrambling. Everything depended on timing in Jill's occupation. She considered herself a master of timing. A pro.

Jewelry was her specialty. Not big stuff, just the flashy items they put into window displays. But if you hit enough middle-class stores without security grilles, and you had a good fence, you could make a living. Not a great living, but a living. The key was perfecting the timing. Even after three years of these thefts, Jill had never been apprehended.

As she sped up the freeway, Jill saw another set of headlights approaching in the outside lane. Before it reached her, the car turned onto an off-ramp.

The police siren sounded a little louder.

Jill was successful because she was willing to work a five- or six-day week like any average bloke. She spent most of that time checking police patrol times and routes around her next hit. She also noted cars that were left out all night in residential areas within ten minutes of her target. She worked out the routes for her getaway and timed them. She allowed herself only one minute for the grab.

That night, Jill had perpetrated her eighteenth hit this year. Shielding her face with the left sleeve of a loose jacket, Jill had swept a standard crowbar across two-thirds of the jewelry store window. In exactly fifty-eight seconds, she'd dropped the crowbar from her gloved hand, slipped her left arm through the necklaces, gathered up bracelets and earrings with her right hand, and dashed back to the idling hot-wired pickup truck. Still carrying the jewelry, with only her left hand free to drive, Jill pulled away from the scene of the crime as the scream of the burglar alarm split the night air.

According to plan, six blocks of normal driving would have brought her to her own car. Six blocks with no stops, at thirty miles per hour. Seventy-two seconds. A minute more and Jill would abandon the stolen vehicle and be quietly away.

But this time, things had not gone according to plan. The

patrol officer she'd watched all week had reversed his pattern that night and came around the corner just as Jill pulled away. The cop had heard the alarm, saw Jill's car and took off after her. Jill hit the gas, twisting and turning at each block. She had to get to her own car without the officer seeing it clearly.

Jill had stolen the pickup six blocks from the dark residential area where she'd left the Chevy halfway up a two-block hill. She made an abrupt U-turn as she approached her own vehicle, facing the truck downhill toward the oncoming police car. She opened the driver's door, gunned the accelerator and jumped out running. Slamming into her own car, she dumped the jewelry on the passenger seat and turned the key she'd left in the ignition. The Chevy roared into action just as the police car turned the corner and confronted the stolen pickup coming at him.

One quick look back in the rearview mirror assured Jill this policeman wouldn't follow her. She watched his car glance off the accelerating truck and careen over the curb and into a crepe myrtle tree. The odd angle of collision had twisted the police car door open and the officer hung halfway out, held only by his seat belt. He wasn't moving.

So there she was, at three in the morning, going the wrong way on the freeway. Jill was sure the police wouldn't chase her on the freeway. They'd try to cut her off and get to her at an exit ramp. No hundred-miles-per-hour, wrong-way chases for them, you could bet!

Again, headlights loomed up ahead. The high beams blinded her so she couldn't tell which lane the car was in. Jill stuck to the middle lane. The speedometer wavered around one hundred. This time, Jill felt a little warm. *What the hell lane is that car in?* she wondered. Half a second later, it flashed by in the fast lane to Jill's right.

The siren was definitely louder.

Glancing in her rearview mirror, she could see the flashing red and blue lights of a patrol car behind her. Not on the freeway but on the surface street that paralleled it. They were trying to get ahead of her, but they didn't know Jill or the Chevy's power.

She pushed her foot to the floorboard and the Chevy jumped, roaring as it gathered speed. One-ten, one-fifteen, one-twenty. *Ha*, thought Jill, *let's see the patrol car do that on a surface street, where it had to contend with intersections and stoplights.*

A second siren penetrated the roar of the engine. Ahead? To her left? Her right? Two? Three? She couldn't tell.

At two miles a minute, even Jill's steady hand couldn't keep the Chevy from shimmying slightly as it took a curve that would have been easy at normal speeds.

Around that curve, Jill was confronted with two pairs of head-lights. *Keep to the middle lane*, Jill thought. *Let the bastards miss **me**.* One car was in the outside lane and the other in the fast, inside lane. But the car to Jill's right didn't stay there, it moved into the center lane ahead of Jill, a half mile away or less. Then it moved back into its original lane. *What the hell is he doing*? thought Jill. *Can't he make up his damn mind? If he comes back again, we've both had it!*

At a three-miles-a-minute closing speed, there's little oppor-tunity for timing.

Jill held the center lane; there was nowhere else for her to go. The car to her right began to pull back into the middle lane just as Jill's Chevy came abreast of it.

But at three-miles-a-minute *parting* speed, a hundredth of a second was all that was necessary for the cars to miss.

Police sirens were wailing all around her now. She figured these weren't the same sirens she'd heard before. No police ve-hicle on a surface street could have come close to staying with her. They'd probably radioed for assistance. Jill suspected that somewhere ahead a roadblock had already been set up across all lanes. Now was the time to choose a ramp.

Jill eased up on the accelerator. The speedometer settled back down, shivered as it passed eighty-seven, and became steady again at eighty. Seventy. Sixty-five. Forty. There was a ramp coming up. The police would expect her to be miles ahead by now. The only sirens she heard were those farther up the road, where surface-street patrol cars might just about be reaching the roadblock.

By the time they realized she'd eluded their trap, she'd be miles and miles in the opposite direction, driving at normal speed in a car none of them had seen well enough to identify.

Jill made a sharp left turn off the freeway and stopped at the sign at the bottom. It was a quiet intersection in a residential area. Not a light showed in a house or a car moved on the street. She pulled the Chevy into a left turn, heading south.

In the middle of the intersection, Jill realized the Chevy was listing slightly; the left front tire was going flat. She must have run over something on the freeway. Good thing she'd slowed down when she did. Jill didn't even want to think about having a flat tire at a hundred and twenty miles an hour.

Quickly, she pulled to the curb, dragged the jack and spare tire from the Chevy's trunk and set about changing the flat. She was even efficient at that. In three minutes, she dropped the jack from under the front axle and threw it and the tire into the trunk.

At that moment, a seedy-looking man in a dirty brown overcoat and a hat pulled low over his eyes stepped out of the bushes and pointed a gun directly at Jill's heart. Jill frowned at the man.

"Listen, this car sure isn't worth stealing."

The man glanced at the car, not knowing the treasure it held in the passenger seat.

"I'm not interested in the car, lady. Just toss me your purse."

Jill thought about that for a second. She had nearly a thousand dollars in her purse, the proceeds from last week's heist. She hated to give up a whole week's work.

As Jill leaped for the car door, a shot rang out.

The gunman stepped closer and peered at her still body and the puddle of blood seeping into the street. He turned and surveyed the neighborhood. It remained dark.

He shrugged. Wasn't it great for him and sad for society that people never wanted to get involved? He reached down, grabbed

Jill by the shoulders and dragged her into the bushes. He hadn't wanted to kill anyone, just steal some money. He hadn't wanted the car, either, but now it would get him away from the body.

He could hear a police siren floating on the air but never dreamed it had anything to do with him or his victim. He pulled the car keys from the trunk lock and swung open the driver's door as a patrol car rolled down the off-ramp and threw a spotlight on the Chevy.

Out of the corner of his eye, the man saw something flash inside the car. He turned his head to stare in disbelief at the pile of jewelry on the seat, sparkling in the beam of light from the police car.

JINX BEERS says that her twenty years spent in Traffic Safety Research, fifteen of them studying the problem of the wrong-way driver, led to the basic concept of this tale. Her goal was to create a story by stringing together events to account for the actions of a delinquent driver. She edits an ongoing anthology, *LSF: Lesbian Short Fiction*, and is writing a mystery novel set at Santa Anita Racetrack.

Nothing Now Can Ever Come to Any Good

Torene Svitil

I should have paid more attention. Had I known that I was making love to Jack for the final time that morning last May, I would have scored each detail into my memory, so that in lonely times I could play them back like a favorite song.

Afterward, Jack left for his daily run, and I drifted back to sleep. I was still asleep when the phone rang.

"Nan? It's Jack." It was Carla Snow, our family doctor.

"What's the matter? Is he okay?"

"I'm so sorry, Nan. Jack collapsed in Griffith Park about an hour ago. Diana Biederman, the city council candidate, saw him fall and called the paramedics. I was here when they brought him in. He died before reaching the hospital."

I could barely hear her over the pounding in my ears. Dread churned my bowels. "No!" I wanted to scream. "I don't believe you." My throat tightened. I could only manage a feeble "What?"

"Jack's dead, Nan."

"But he's in great shape. He runs every day. Just this morning—" I protested and stopped, trying to recall the touch of Jack's hands on my body. "How could it happen?"

"He was fifty-two, Nan. He seems to have had a heart attack. A lot of men that age do. Apparently, he also hit his head pretty badly when he fell down the hill."

Trembling uncontrollably, I managed to croak, "I want to see him."

"He's at Hollywood Presbyterian. A coroner still needs to examine him. I'll wait here until you come. Get someone to drive you."

I put down the receiver, shocked to see that by the clock it had taken barely two minutes for my life to change forever. I had thought the phrase "broken heart" was metaphorical, but my hands and feet were icy, as if my heart were so damaged that it could no longer pump my blood that far. It took three tries to dial my sister Ellen; I couldn't make sense of the numbers. Somehow my frozen lips moved, forming the words. I could hear the tears in her voice, but my eyes stayed dry.

The sun was shining when we left the hospital with Jack's things stuffed into a plastic bag. Luminous jacaranda blossoms carpeted the streets. We walked to the car, past people absorbed in mundane tasks. Numbed by the ether of grief, I was denied the comfort of ordinary activity.

When we reached the house, Ellen pulled into the driveway and shut off the engine. "Are you going to be okay?" She put her arm around my shoulders and squeezed tight.

I nodded automatically.

"Well, at least Diana Biederman wasn't at the hospital acting all sympathetic in front of the press. I can't believe she missed a chance to show her caring side, especially so close to the election. I don't think she's missed so much as a ribbon-cutting since she entered politics." Ellen stopped suddenly, worn out by her one-sided effort to carry on a normal conversation. "Want some company?" she asked.

"No thanks, sweetie. Maybe I'll call you later, but right now, I'd like to be alone for a while."

Waving goodbye, I walked into the house to face my solitary future. In the hallway hung the black-and-white portrait of Jack that I had shot as a present for his fiftieth birthday. I stroked the familiar, kind, broad face. I was sure that, if I simply focused hard enough, I could pull his essence from the things he touched, from the floors he walked across, and spin his substance from the elements.

Taking an old photo album from the bookshelf, I drifted into the bedroom and slipped into the hollow his body had made in the rumpled bed as if I were nestling into his arms.

Jack and I met during a protest march in San Francisco in the seventies. The photos from that day show me in full hippie regalia: flowers woven through long, almost-blond curls, camera aimed at the crowd. Even then, I saw the world through a viewfinder. Jack sported a beard and long hair tied back with a headband. In his right hand, an angry placard demanded an end to the war.

After the march dispersed, we joined a group of protesters at a nearby coffeehouse. Hours after everyone else left, we were still talking. About the only thing we didn't talk about was Vietnam.

I didn't learn he was a vet until the first night we spent together, when I asked about the scar that creased his buttock. Despite my diffident questions, all he would say was that he got it in the war. Once, later, he told me about an untried officer who, maddened by rain, exhaustion and killing, by the fear that echoed from the hills, turned against his own men. A couple of times, I tried to get him to talk about it, but the last thing he wanted was to remember.

So, most of what I learned about that time came from observation—his compulsion for order, his passion for justice, his rigid sense of right and wrong. We lived with ants every summer because, he said, he'd seen what chemicals could do to people.

A photo, loosened from its mounts, slipped out of the album. In it, Jack, the grunt, preened for the camera with three buddies— audacious, pumped and young in a way they would never be again. That picture was Jack's sole tangible reminder of the war, apart from his scar. He called it his memento mori: Of the four, he alone made it out alive.

By way of a eulogy, I read the names written on the back: Too Loose, holding his helmet over his crotch and laughing; skinny, adolescent Gigi, flashing the peace sign; Meech, the cowboy, a bucking bronc tattooed over his heart; and Jack, dangling a cigarette from his lips.

I stuck the photo back on the page and turned to a happier image—our wedding day. Early morning sun lit a dusty bar where, giddy with love, we hoisted celebratory beers.

One month after we met, Jack and I piled into a Volkswagen van with four friends and drove all night across the state line to Nevada. We were married by a justice of the peace in a small desert town shortly after the sun came up. As time passed, we became less giddy, but no less in love with each other.

I buried my nose in the pillow and inhaled Jack's musky scent, but try as I might, I couldn't visualize his face. As soon as I looked away from the photographs, he vanished from my mind's eye. It was the ultimate loss.

Much later, I awoke from a troubled sleep. In my dream, Jack walked through the front door. I rushed to kiss him, but there was only emptiness where his face should have been. Grasping his shoulders, I tried to pull him to me. From beneath us rose a horrible, keening moan, and he was gone.

I lay there without moving for quite a while. Street lights blazed through the uncurtained windows, not quite bright enough to eliminate the shadows lurking in the corners. I got up, pulled the curtains shut and switched on the bedside lamp.

Then I reached for the phone. "Nan," Carla answered groggily. "What's the matter?"

"Tell me again where Jack was found?"

"Griffith Park. Why?"

"He never ran in the park."

"Well, he did today. Or do I mean yesterday?"

I looked at the clock. It was two A.M. "I'm sorry, Carla. I didn't realize it was so late." I inhaled deeply and let the breath out. "Jack was obsessive. He always ran the exact same route.

Always. He never even reversed direction. You're positive he was in the park?"

"Nan, the police found blood on the rocks where Jack hit his head. Can we talk about this in the morning?"

"Okay," I said reluctantly. Suddenly, I was hungry for details. How had Jack died? Why had he died where he did? "Carla, was it the fall that killed him?"

"We'll know for sure in a few days."

"But wouldn't you have spotted heart trouble during his physical?"

"Not necessarily. His heart could have been clogged with this stuff like Jell-O. It wouldn't show up during a general exam. Nan, please try to get some sleep. Do you need sleeping pills or Valium?"

"I'll be okay. I'll call you in the morning."

I paced and drank coffee and paced some more, waiting for the sun to rise. At six, I dressed quickly in shorts and sweatshirt and left the house, carrying a recent photo of Jack.

I'm not a good runner. After we bought the house in Los Feliz a year earlier, I had jogged with Jack a few times but stopped when an old knee injury flared up. Still, I had traveled the route with him often enough to have memorized each step. Like everything else he did, the course was carefully planned: precisely three miles, round trip, with an aerobic balance between hills and flat stretches.

A cacophony of bird song assaulted the morning. Fighting an irrational anger at life for continuing in Jack's absence, I started up the hill. Everywhere, election posters decorated lawns and windows. As if to remind me of my loss, most flaunted Diana Biederman's name.

I knew Jack must have met the same people, day after day, as they walked their dogs or weeded their lawns. Someone must have seen him yesterday. Someone who could help me patch together the steps that had led to his death.

After a quarter mile, I passed a young woman doing leg stretches. I showed her Jack's picture. "Sure, I've seen him lots of times. Kind of a tall guy with a little belly?" She gave me a funny look. "What's he done?"

"Nothing. He's my husband. He died suddenly while he was jogging. Maybe this sounds weird to you, but I think I'd feel better if I knew exactly what happened."

Her expression changed. "Oh gosh, I'm sorry. I can't help you, though. I don't run every day, and I wasn't out yesterday. I'm so sorry." She reached out sympathetically and patted my arm.

"Thanks, anyway," I said and urged my reluctant legs onward. My lungs ached. Jack made this run easily every day. It didn't make sense. I passed a white-haired woman walking a little white dog, one of those yappy breeds, and gratefully slowed down.

"Excuse me. I wonder if you saw this man running here yesterday?" Her dog started to growl.

"Shut up, Baxter," she said and tugged on his leash. "He's really friendly but he acts macho to make up for his size, don't you, baby?" she cooed at the dog. Baxter sniffed my sneakers and fixed me with his beady eyes.

She peered at the photo. "Oh, sure. He was one of the regulars. You get to know all their schedules after a while. I'm here every day with Baxter, rain or shine. Dogs need to go out even if you don't feel like taking them."

"Did you see him yesterday?"

"Yesterday? I'm sure I did. Why? Did something happen to him?"

"He died during his run."

"Dead? He was so young. Of course, most people seem young to me. I'm seventy-five." Interest shone from her eyes.

"My husband was a creature of habit," I explained. "You saw him every morning, so you know what I mean. Yet for some reason, he was in Griffith Park when he collapsed yesterday."

"Heart attack?"

"Probably."

"Oh, you poor thing. My Frankie died of a heart attack. It's the best way, though, don't you think? They don't suffer for long."

"What time was it when you saw him?"

"It would have been about six-thirty. I take Baxter out from six-thirty to seven every morning."

So he had come at least this far yesterday. I continued retracing Jack's steps, but returned home without learning anything else.

The next couple of mornings, I kept to Jack's schedule. Faces started to look familiar to me. I guess I was becoming one of the regulars.

"Nan, you've got to stop this." I was sitting in Carla Snow's examination room. After she learned about my daily jogs, she insisted that I come in for a checkup, saying that she didn't want two patients to drop dead on her. Running a hand through her short red curls, she continued her lecture. "For whatever reason, Jack was jogging a different route when he died. Adults are allowed to change their minds. Jack died a natural death. I think that this investigation, or whatever you call it, is your attempt to hold onto him. It's not healthy."

"Maybe you're right, Carla, but 'rigid' was Jack's middle name. Whenever we moved to a new city, the first thing he did was work out a running course, and he never changed it."

"Hmmm." Carla folded her stethoscope into her lab coat pocket. "Well, your heart sounds fine. The exercise may help you sleep better, but it won't be good for your knees. As I told Jack many times, jogging is bad for you. I recommend that my middle-aged patients ride bikes or walk or swim rather than run."

That did it. I now was determined to prove that I could do anything with my middle-aged body that I could have done with my twenty-year-old one. I slipped down from the examination table, but Carla didn't leave, as she usually did, to allow me to dress in private. She perched on the lone chair in the room. "Don't take this the wrong way," she began. "I wonder if you knew Jack as well as you think you did."

"Why do you say that?"

"Something was bothering him. He alluded to it the last time

I saw him. Did he tell you what it was?"

"No." Doubt flickered in my mind. "Was he worried about his health?"

"He asked me, as a Catholic, for my thoughts on confession. I'm afraid I gave him that old platitude about it being good for the soul. That was that. But think back. Had you noticed anything unusual about his behavior? Did he seem preoccupied? Did he get strange phone calls?"

"If you're thinking that he was having an affair, you're wrong. I'd know. We made love that morning." A ghastly thought occurred to me. "Could that have put extra stress on Jack's heart?"

Eyeing me seriously, Carla asked, "Is that why you've been jarring your bones on the pavement?"

"Maybe a little."

"Well, stop. Do something normal like crying."

Fat chance. At night, I tried to make myself cry, but my eyes wouldn't cooperate. There was nothing inside to come out as tears; I was simply hollow.

The next morning, I was back on the street. As I started up the first hill, a sharp pain shot through my kneecap—that old injury. Despite Carla's hints, I knew I was right about Jack, but she was right about my middle-aged body. I would have to try another approach.

I started knocking on doors. At the tenth house, a pleasant, blue Colonial, I came face to face with Diana Biederman. I had forgotten that she lived so close. She was quietly gorgeous, with dark wavy hair to her shoulders, large, limpid brown eyes with long eyelashes, and a rosy complexion to which no photograph or TV camera had ever done justice.

"My name is Nan Howard," I began. "I understand that you called the paramedics after my husband collapsed the other day. Will you tell me about it?"

She didn't speak for a long minute. "I don't see what good that would do."

Nearby, a leaf blower began a deafening roar. "Please," I

bellowed over the din. "I won't take much of your time. It's so hard for me because I wasn't there when he died."

"He was unconscious when I found him. I honestly can't help you," she repeated.

"But it would help me to talk to you," I insisted.

After another long, silent pause, she glanced at her watch and said, "I have a little time."

I held out my hand. She barely touched my fingers and stepped aside. "Come in," she said without warmth. I followed her through a door off the hallway into a room that functioned as an office.

I didn't like Diana Biederman, the politician. She had a tendency to moralize, painting herself as the arbiter of ethical behavior, while not averse to a few dirty tricks of her own. During her school board race, she had capitalized on an opponent's youthful misstep, distorting it until he seemed to be akin to the anti-Christ. All's fair if you believe you're on the side of the righteous, I guess. Now I had met Diana Biederman, the woman, and I didn't much like her, either.

"What do you want to ask me?" she demanded.

As I had so many times recently, I drew a picture of Jack's obsessive nature. "That's why I was so surprised that you saw him in the park," I concluded.

She shrugged. "Maybe he got bored. How do you know he hadn't been running there before?"

"I knew my husband."

"Does any woman really know her husband?"

This was so similar to what Carla Snow had asked that I was taken aback for a moment. "What do you mean?"

"Just that you can live with someone for years, thinking that you have a good marriage, and then something comes straight out of the blue and knocks you cold."

Was she speaking from personal experience? Without responding, I waited for her to continue.

"I often walk in the park in the morning," she began. "As I was coming down a hill, I saw your husband stumble and fall off the trail. He was unconscious and his breath was ragged, so I used my cell phone to call 9-1-1." She grimaced, as if distressed by the memory.

"Had you ever seen Jack there before?"

"I doubt I would have noticed him. I use the time to work out difficult problems or things that are bothering me. I don't pay much attention to what's going on around me."

The phone rang. "Would you excuse me?" Diana Biederman asked. "It's probably my husband. He's been out of town. I won't be long."

I took the opportunity to glance around the office. It was small and arranged for efficiency rather than comfort. Her desk was empty, except for a neat stack of papers, a calendar, an ashtray and the phone. A bookcase filled with law and other reference books lined one wall. The single personal touch was a photograph of her with her husband.

He had stayed in the background during her campaign, never appearing in public with her, as if unwilling to shift the spotlight from politics to her personal life. I knew Biederman was her maiden name, but his name escaped me; he'd made no more of an impression on me than most male politicians' wives. I did remember that his money had helped elect her to the school board. I studied his face.

He appeared to be in his late forties or early fifties. He might have been handsome except for a cast in his right eye and a swath of scar tissue above his right ear that pulled his features into a frozen smirk. Maybe that was why he kept such a low profile.

Diana Biederman's conversation caught my ear. "I lost you for a second," I heard her say. "Are you in the car? Great. Get home as soon as you can. I'm with the wife of the man in Griffith Park. Missed you, too."

I think I knew then.

She put down the phone and considered me. "If there's nothing more, it's getting late."

I didn't want to leave yet; too much was still unclear. "Have you been married long?" I asked, stalling for time.

She arched an eyebrow. "Ten years. Why?"

"Jack and I were married for twenty-five years. When you live with someone that long, you develop a sixth sense, don't you find?"

"I suppose you could call it that."

"That's what I meant when I said I knew my husband. I didn't know every thought he had. In fact, there was a lot he never told me, especially about his past. We rarely discussed the time he spent in Vietnam, for example, but over the years, I began to understand the ways in which it affected him. Your husband seems to be about the same age as Jack. Was he injured in the war?"

Diana Biederman's shoulders stiffened. "Buck lost the sight of his eye in a hunting accident. He had a medical deferment."

Buck Meecham. The name snapped into my consciousness, and with it, everything came into focus. Meech, the Arizona cowboy. He was terribly changed. But now I was sure.

When I thought I could control my voice, I said, "Jack was wounded in the war. Once, he told me about it. I thought talking would help him put it behind him, but he felt differently. In a way, I could see his point. It was a hard story to forget."

Without taking her eyes from my face, Diana Biederman started to pick at the polish on her thumbnail.

"You may have heard something like it. A young lieutenant sends out a patrol. The jungle is freezing; a cold rain is falling and visibility is poor. There's a short burst of gunfire. Then the screaming starts, high and thin. Over the screams, a Viet Cong sniper taunts the men in camp. It means death to go after their dying pal. No one does. The screams become moans; the time between them becomes longer. Finally, they stop.

"The men try to sleep. Sometime later, there's more gunfire. The lieutenant, tormented by grief and guilt, is firing blindly into the jungle. When a grunt tries to stop him, the lieutenant turns on the soldier and shoots him, point blank, in the chest. He walks back through the bunker, spraying bullets in all directions. The men scramble for their weapons, but he seems invulnerable. Coolly, he surveys the devastation and walks out of camp. There is one last shot in the distance."

Diana Biederman had worked almost all the polish off her nail.

"Jack was lucky. He crawled under one of the bodies. It was late in the morning when the mist cleared enough for a helicopter to land and pick up the survivors. They left without the lieutenant, certain that he was dead. But he wasn't dead, was he?"

"How would I know?" Diana Biederman reached for a cigarette. Her hand shook as she lit it.

"Jack kept a snapshot with his buddies' names written on the back. I'm surprised that your husband still calls himself Buck. As soon as you said it, I remembered the lieutenant's bucking horse tattoo and his full name. Your husband's altered, but he still resembles that young soldier. What happened when Jack recognized him?"

With a steadier hand, Diana Biederman squashed her unsmoked cigarette in the ashtray. When she looked up, a tear trickled photogenically down her cheek. "He did it for me," she said, watching my reaction. "He knew the story would hurt me politically. I heard it for the first time a few weeks ago. Until your husband confronted him, Buck had no idea that anyone had survived. He went into the jungle that night hoping to die, but the Viet Cong captured him. He lived—after a fashion. He's paid a thousand times over for what he did."

In the background, a door closed. Footsteps approached the office where I sat with Diana Biederman. "What did you tell her?" His terse words sounded desperate.

"She knows, Buck."

Meecham stopped somewhere behind me. I was afraid to turn around. "It was finally going so well for us," he said. The edge was gone from his voice. He spoke in a monotone, as if the words had no meaning. "Diana's career was taking off. People supported her and what she stood for. If only I hadn't left for work so early that day. I saw Jack. I knew him right away, but I didn't think he recognized me. The next day, he was waiting for me."

Diana Biederman pursed her lips, as if making a difficult decision. Her hand crept toward the telephone and eased the receiver up a bit. I twisted in my seat to face her husband. His good eye flickered frantically in its socket. Every muscle in his face was tight with tension. One fist clutched a jagged granite paperweight. I wished I could see inside his head. "Why did you kill him?" I asked.

"He wouldn't leave us alone. He wanted me to confess. Confess. I suffered for over twenty-five years. Wasn't that enough? Jack always was a self-righteous asshole. Why should our lives be ruined for something that happened a lifetime ago? He kept asking why I should have a life when all those others didn't. Shit, the V.C. would have gotten most of them, anyway. I saved them from dying like that other poor fuck. That screaming. I still hear it at night."

From behind me came the faint murmur of what I assumed was the 9-1-1 dispatcher. I raised my voice to cover the sound. "Your mistake was taking him to the park after you killed him. I knew something was wrong as soon as I heard he was picked up there. Jack always ran on open streets. He hated the park. The trees weren't beautiful to him. They meant danger. He hated the smell of vegetation and wet soil. He had nightmares, too."

Meecham continued as if I hadn't said a word. "I sat in my own piss in the dark for hours. My wound got infected. Look at my face; I'm blind in one eye. They kicked me, beat me, tortured me. I wanted to die, but they wouldn't let me." Both his eyes were still and dead now. He was no longer in the room with his wife and me, but somewhere black and lonely.

"That wasn't enough punishment to suit Jack." He took a step toward us, raising the paperweight. "I didn't want to kill him. I just wanted him to shut up." He slammed the paperweight into his open palm.

Outside, car tires screeched on the pavement. The sound didn't register on Meecham's face. He was past caring.

"So you hit him to keep him quiet." My whole body shook with rage, but I tried to keep my voice calm. Behind Meecham, a uniformed officer slipped through the half-open door.

"I didn't want to kill him," Meecham repeated, "but he crumpled as soon as I hit him. He didn't bleed very much. He shouldn't have died."

"Turn around, sir. Hold your hands away from your body and turn around." Meecham's expression didn't change. He did as he was told. The cop took the chunk of rock from his unresisting hand and cuffed him. "You okay, Ms. Biederman?" At her abrupt nod, he hustled her husband away. Her face twisted with genuine agony.

A second officer stood right inside the door. Diana Biederman closed her eyes and sat still until she regained her composure. "Please leave now," she ordered.

The cop moved forward. "If I could get some information from you two ladies first."

"You would have let him get away with murder." I couldn't keep the loathing out of my voice.

"I love him." She looked directly at me. "Surely you of all people can understand that."

"You're as guilty of killing Jack as he is."

"He should have kept quiet," she said reproachfully. "Anyway, I tried to save his life. I'm the one who called the paramedics."

"You could have called an ambulance from here. But if Jack had lived, your husband would have gone to jail, and the scandal would have destroyed your political career. I think you took Jack to the park so that it would look like an accident, and then you waited until he was dead."

"He was breathing when the paramedics came," Diana Biederman said. "But I'm not sorry he died. I tried to protect Buck. I sent him out of town. I thought it would all work out. Who would doubt that a man that age had died of a heart attack?" She rose and walked over to where the officer stood waiting. "Now maybe Buck will get the help he needs."

"Do you think turning him in will save your career?" I asked scornfully.

As I brushed past her, she stopped me. "Buck has suffered, you know. People might have understood about what happened there—many men broke down under those conditions—but he's never forgiven himself. And neither had your husband."

Several hours later, I walked through my front door and stood in front of Jack's picture. There was death in those eyes; I had just refused to see it before. Diana Biederman was right: Jack had never forgiven himself for surviving. He had asked Meecham why he deserved to live when the others were dead. It must have been a question he asked himself all the time. By confronting him, Jack had tried to put an end to his anguish over a past that wouldn't stay past, no matter how hard he tried to control it. And I had been wrong: I didn't know my husband.

I examined his face, seeing it unfiltered by sentiment as if for the first time. Without warning, tears blurred his image; but when I closed my eyes, I saw Jack as clearly as if he were in the room with me. I started to cry.

TORENE SVITIL has written feature articles and film criticism for numerous publications, including the *New York Times, Screen International* and the *Los Angeles Times,* before turning her efforts to mystery fiction. She is currently working on a novel about a tabloid reporter accused of murdering her boyfriend's ex-wife.

L.A. Justice

Kris Neri

I've come to expect the unexpected from my parents. After decades of being billed as "Hollywood's madcap couple," those loveable loonies, Martha Collins and Alec Grainger, wouldn't recognize the real world if it bit them. But Mother's doozy of a pre-dawn telephone call surprised even me.

"Tracy!" she hissed. "There's a man in my bed."

Now I ask you, is that something a mother should say to her impressionable thirty-four-year-old child? I told her as much.

I might have been less flippant had I known the man was dead.

With Dad away on location and their latest housekeeper having quit, I'd anticipated frequent appeals from Mother, only I figured they'd be more mundane. You'd think I'd learn. I broke countless laws racing from my Studio City condo to their Beverly Hills home and arrived to find Mother waiting in the open doorway. Seeing her fighting back tears, I wanted to take her in my arms and kiss the hurt away like she used to do for me—until I realized it wasn't the presence of the dead guy that upset her.

"Tracy, darling," she mourned, "you're not dressed."

Stealing a glance to make sure that in my haste I hadn't left the house naked, I saw that I was wearing my favorite battered sweats, just as I thought. Mother, of course, was decked out well enough to appear on *The Tonight Show*. To say our standards differ is the understatement of the century.

"Excuse me, Mother. I didn't know that finding a stiff in your bed constituted a formal affair."

Still, I might have popped for underwear if death had come calling at a saner hour. I'm not a morning person in the best of times, but with my husband, Drew, out of town for some lawyer-do, I severed the scant hold the nine-to-five world has on me and frittered the night away sucking down Häagen-Dazs and taking in a *Remington Steele* marathon. I'd had less than an hour's sleep when that panicky call came through.

"Mother, forget about me. Who died? How—" I caught sight of the living room through the open archway. Every piece of furniture had been knocked over and torn apart. "What did you do? Host your last tornado or wrap party here?"

"That's how I found it. It's how the whole house looks."

So someone had been searching for something. My hope that this might just be a practical joke was starting to seem foolish. I raced up the stairs to the master bedroom.

Nope, no one was laughing. Tossed on the bed like a rag-doll in a dumpster was a twenty-something man. Despite an unfortunate tendency toward flashy clothes, he must have been a looker before someone blew off the top of his head and death turned his skin a trifle pasty. The proverbial tall, dark and handsome, if it isn't too tacky to check out a corpse.

"Well, there's nothing we can do but call the police."

Mother's martyred sigh overflowed with exasperation. "Tracy, *I* could have done that. Why do you think I called you?"

I knew why. Because she bought into the myth that I, as a mystery writer, could solve cases on my own. Don't laugh—I believed it, too. But still, real people can't operate like the amateur detectives in books. Or so Drew kept telling me.

"Tracy, if you call the police, they're sure to put your old mother in jail."

She only refers to herself as "old" when she wants something, so I didn't take her seriously. "Why would they do that? You couldn't have known this clown."

"Oh, but I did," she insisted. "Paolo Luca was my...protégé."

"Your...? Oh God! Do you mean to tell me that while my father is slaving away on some remote location shoot, you're messing around with a kid a quarter of your age?"

"Half!"

We compromised on a third. "But you've given him money?"

Reluctant nod. "And that van we had. I was even planning to take him to Cannes with me next week. Oh, you wouldn't understand."

I understood, all right. She paid a young man to flatter her, to make her feel young. And I thought all the old fools were men.

"Jeez, Mother." I spotted a gun tossed on the floor.

"Don't pick it up!"

"The idea never occurred to me. What idiot—" Oops, I thought, looking into the face of Fury. "Don't tell me you haven't played the patsy in enough pictures to know you *never*—"

"You're obviously confusing me with some B-movie queen."

Right.

"Besides, it's my gun. My fingerprints must be on it. I practiced at the range just yesterday."

"You have a gun? I'm a mystery writer and I don't have one. Are you any good?"

"Crack shot."

"Really? I've always figured I'd close my eyes and—"

"Tracy, aren't we getting off track?"

It's called denial. I absently slumped onto the bed; before leaping away, my hand brushed Paolo's.

"He's warmer than I am."

"I don't think he'd been...you know—when I came home."

"But you must have an alibi. Where were you at this hour?"

"At Franny's."

Terrific. You might remember Francesca Grant. She played

the secondary lead in a few of Mother's pictures. They have dinner together about once a month and watch tapes of their old movies. Too bad she has Alzheimer's. By morning, Franny wouldn't remember how many toes she had.

"We fell asleep in front of the set. When I woke up, I put a blanket over Franny and left."

"Franny's companion?"

"Already asleep in her room."

That hole Mother was in just kept getting deeper. I glared at the cause. "Where did you pick up old Paolo?"

"Don't make it sound sordid. I met him through his uncle, Antonio, a charming gentleman and quite good-looking for his age."

That meant he was at least ten years younger than she was.

"It was all very proper, Tracy."

"As long as you overlook that dead boy-toy on your— Wait a minute. Paolo's uncle isn't Antonio *Luca*, is he? Hangs around Folio's Ristorante downtown?"

"He is there a lot."

"No! Don't you read the papers? Antonio Luca is reputed to be the most notorious crime boss on the West Coast."

"There is no mob in L.A. Everyone knows that."

"Fine. You wanna tell him, or should I?"

Talk about giving new meaning to the rock-and-a-hard-place squeeze. At least, the cops would ask questions; Luca's crowd wasn't known for due process.

"Uh, darling. I'm afraid you haven't heard the worst."

"It can't get any worse, Mother," I snapped.

"When I came home, there was a message on the machine from your father. They've changed his shooting schedule. He'll be home later this week, instead of next month. In time to go with me to Cannes."

So she not only wanted me to do the impossible, she wanted it fast. For once, Mother withered under my glare. Biting her lip indecisively, stripped of all her protective affectations—I had her right where I'd always wanted her. It broke my heart. Despite the stormy roller coaster she insisted on making of their marriage, she adored Dad. And so did I. What choice did I have?

I still longed to taunt her, to demand how she would have coped with both Paolo and Dad at Cannes. But what would be the point? Consequence was too abstract a concept for Mother to deal with when life was tickling her nose. Maybe some people really are so far outside the norm that they can't be held to conventional standards.

I'd have to remember that for my own defense when Drew lowered the boom on me.

I finally agreed to put Paolo on ice. Literally. Mother's neighbor was away and had left an emergency key with my parents. Happily, she had a walk-in freezer.

"How are we going to get him there, Tracy?"

I wanted to throw him over the fence, but she wouldn't hear of it. Since Paolo had thoughtfully left the van in the driveway before buying country real estate, I said we'd take that and asked her for the keys.

"I don't have them, dear. I gave Paolo the only set."

"So get them."

"I'm not going to touch him—you get them."

"Oh, for chrissakes."

I patted Paolo down, but there weren't any keys in his pockets now. Figured. If his killer hadn't found what he was looking for there, he'd try Paolo's place. I ordered Mother to get over her squeamishness and help me drag Paolo to the van. He wasn't a small man and he was starting to like the position he'd been left in too much to change.

"But, darling, how will you start the van without keys?"

"Don't worry, I'll hot-wire it."

She shot me a look across the bow of her "protégé." "Surely a response to warm any mother's heart. Don't even tell me where you picked up that little skill."

I hate it when she acts like a normal mother. Who was she trying to kid? She hadn't winced at making me an accessory.

We wrestled Paolo into the back of the van. The engine started up as easily as my parents' cars always had when I was in high school and they refused to let me borrow them.

"Oh, Tracy, where did I go wrong? How did you develop this skewed sense of right and wrong?"

My tongue still hurts where I bit it.

"What would your father think?"

I thought she had a lot of nerve bringing Dad into it, considering what was decomposing just a few feet behind us. But maybe she really felt lost in this crisis without him. They had been together through a lot of married years. For that matter, they were together when they were divorced, and even, let's face it—when they were married to other people.

Now, I was thrilled Drew wasn't there to witness this caper. He was too much the Officer-of-the-Court to condone our turning The Victim into a popsicle. If he ever learned of it, there would be no living with him. Doubtless a moot point, since Mother and I were unlikely to emerge from this skirmish in any better shape than Paolo.

"I could sure use a drink," Mother announced after we left Paolo in his new home.

"Don't get comfortable, Mother. We're only half finished." I reminded her that we still had to put the house in order. "If either the police or the mob drops by, this place has to look like nothing happened here."

Mother affected a yawn. "Tracy, dear, you know how much I'd love to help, but when a woman reaches my age, she needs her sleep. You'll understand someday."

I understood now—she was sticking me with a mess second only to the one left by the Northridge earthquake. I spent hours cleaning that place and burning the bedspread in the fireplace. Finally, I took the shower I so desperately needed and found myself standing knee-deep in water that wouldn't drain.

While I leaned over the side of the tub, with Drano corroding my hands as I wrestled with the drain cover, Mother appeared in the doorway wearing a satin negligee and an honest-to-God feather boa.

"Mother, you're awake. I can't tell you how much I miss the privileged life of a celebrity child."

"If you cursed quieter, I wouldn't be. For a sweet young thing, you sure have a smutty mouth."

"Yeah, yeah. Get me a screwdriver, will ya?"

"Where might something like that be?" she asked.

"Never mind. I've got it." No wonder the water wouldn't drain. Stuffed down the pipe was a narrow cloth bag that had to be over a foot long. "Unless you've taken to hiding things in your plumbing, this must be what Paolo's killer was looking for." I ripped open the stitches at the top and dumped some of the contents into my hand. What a disappointment. "Who would hide this? It's just a bag of gravel."

Mother laughed, a trifle hysterically. "Gravel. Darling, those aren't stones—they're uncut diamonds."

"Diamonds?" I rolled one around in my hand.

"Good ones, too, by the looks of them. There must be over a hundred of them, each as big as your eyeballs."

I'd heard organized crime frequently converted large amounts of cash into diamonds for easier movement across borders. Bet I knew whose suitcase had been targeted to carry them to Cannes. How could I tell her it was a set-up?

"Are you thinking what I'm thinking?" Mother asked.

Maybe she figured it out herself.

"I don't know," I said cautiously. "What are you thinking?"

"How we'll wow them at the next Academy Awards."

Funny, I was wondering who my real parents were.

"Tell me again why we're doing this?" Mother asked when I parked near Folio's Ristorante. "If you ask me, we should be as far away from this place as possible."

"I already told you. You're going to go in there and give the performance of your life so—"

"Oh, this won't be the performance of my life. That would be either—"

"Mother! You have to convince Luca you don't know where Paolo is, so they look *elsewhere* for him."

"Oh. And why are you riding shotgun?"

"Because there's a good chance someone in Luca's circle will know you're lying, and I'm counting on reading that thought on his face."

Now I understood how Paolo had conned Mother. If he was anything like his uncle, the boy had been smooth. Of course, it may not have been passed by either genes or association. Luca introduced us to his son, Denny, and one of his "boys," Tom Ricci.

Denny was like a big, dumb dog, eager to please his old man, but clumsy. The way his tongue lolled on his drooping lower lip, he even looked like a panting dog. But Ricci bore watching. While he was as flashy and as much a stereotypical thug as Paolo had been, right down to the ornate pinkie rings, I saw unexpected depth in his dark eyes.

"Always a pleasure to see you, Martha, and to meet your charming daughter, but I thought you would be with Paolo," Luca said in his exquisite accent.

"You mean Paolo isn't here?" Concern tugged at Mother's features. "Oh, dear. I hope nothing has happened to him. We were planning a trip. To Cannes, you know."

I caught the look that passed between Luca and his henchmen. They knew very well.

"When Paolo didn't return my calls, naturally I thought—" Her voice caught.

I could see the wheels turning in Luca's eyes. They were his diamonds, all right.

"Now, Pop, don't jump to no conclusions. You know Paolo

knew how much this trip to Cannes meant to…uh…him," Denny ended stupidly. "He wouldn't just take off."

While Denny and Luca went through the charade of speculating where Paolo might be, strictly for our benefit, Tom studied Mother thoughtfully, like he was trying to place this new piece into the puzzle. He knew Paolo was dead, I was sure of it.

People, especially those of a certain age who spent their youth idolizing Martha Collins, The Star, will do anything for her. The elderly locksmith who re-keyed her house the last time she blew up at Dad didn't blink at loaning me his picks. I should have held out for a lesson. We thought we were so clever when we tailed Tom Ricci to that flophouse. But if the lock on his door had been any harder to pick, the caper was going to end in that hall with the rats and roaches.

"Hurry, Tracy. Who knows how long he'll be gone."

"Got it!"

Ricci's room surprised me. Not only was it too clean for that dump, there was a monastic simplicity that didn't jibe with his taste in apparel.

"I'll search while you watch the door, Mother. If you see him coming, we'll dive into the closet."

Seemed like a good plan. Too bad one of us couldn't stick to it. She kept coming up behind me and looking over my shoulder. The third time, I was about to chew her out, only she noticed something.

"Oh, look. That drawer has a false bottom. I had a hidden panel like that put into a night table when you were little and liked to snoop through my things."

I remembered that. I used to check it out all the time. I pressed the hidden lever, but it stuck.

"Uh, Tracy…"

"Not now, Mother, I can't get this thing— There it goes."

"Darling," she went on, in her best movie-star tone, "you remember meeting this lovely man, Tom Ricci, don't you?"

I whirled around. Some gatekeeper. Ricci had not only slipped past her, he had also pulled his gun on us. I smiled knowingly and gestured with the wallet I found in the hidden space.

"No, Mother, I remember meeting Special Agent Thomas Ricci of the FBI."

"I don't understand, Tom," Mother said. "What does it mean to be in 'deep cover'?"

Please, tell me I'm adopted.

"Martha, it just means I'm a man without a life."

Talk about sobering remarks. And subtle changes. Tom looked as much the wiseguy as ever, but the honest expression of the real man dominated his appearance now. Along with his pain.

"Tracy, I believed in this when I started, but I don't know who the good guys are anymore. All my superiors seem to care about is nailing Luca. I'm supposed to ignore whatever anyone else does. I've looked the other way so many times, I can't live with myself."

"You knew about Paolo's murder?"

"Sure. I followed Denny to your mom's house."

"Denny?" I'd obviously missed one of those telling expressions. Maybe because Denny's face was as expressive as cheesecake. "Why would he kill Paolo, his own cousin?"

"You've seen what he's like. His old man never trusts him with anything important. Paolo was the heir apparent. Denny probably figured he'd steal Luca's diamonds and branch out on his own, but Paolo outsmarted him."

"Surely now they'll let you out," I insisted. "They'll need your testimony."

He snorted. "You think that was the first murder I've kept quiet about?" Tom insisted he knew of two other murders Paolo committed, and he'd actually helped Denny buy guns, arrange for a bomb and deal drugs. "Maybe if I could have tied Luca to any of it, but..." Tom shrugged. "Look at it from my bosses' perspective. With Paolo gone and Denny so hopeless, I'm going to be worth more to Luca than ever. They'll never let me go now."

"Paolo...? Oh my," Mother murmured.

Tom shook his head. "I've got a wife and kids I hardly ever see, and for what? I tell ya, Tracy, if I had some money, I'd just walk away and start life over somewhere else."

"And so you shall, dear boy," Mother said and patted his hand. "My daughter will make it possible."

Huh? They both looked at me expectantly. Why me? I mean, he was this tough federal cop, hardened by years of deep cover within the mob. Who was I? Just Tracy Eaton, mystery writer and detective wannabe. What did they expect me to do?

"Tom, I know you're sick of duplicity, but...well, how do you feel about shell games?"

Tom's eyes brightened. "Tracy, you find me a big enough shell and I'll be glad to be your pea."

It's hard to feel like you're commanding a well-trained army when your troops act more like the Keystone Kops. If it had been fun lugging Paolo down the stairs, rescuing him from the neighbor's freezer after he took shape, so to speak, was too many laughs for me. Do frozen corpses weigh more, or was I just getting really sick of Paolo?

"Hold up your end, Mother. If he hits the driveway, you're picking up the pieces."

"Tracy, really—how callous. The dead deserve our respect," that maternal paragon insisted.

Like it had been my idea to stash him. My offensive imagery seemed to do the trick, however. Mother developed surprising strength for an old lady, slipping Paolo into the van like he'd been greased.

"I still don't see why we had to move him," she grumbled after we tucked the van back in her yard. "You saw how little Myrna keeps in that freezer. She might not have found him for years."

Mother was obviously being respectful to the dead again. And as forgetful as ever.

"The objective isn't to delay the discovery of the murder, it's to shatter all connection with you. To muddy the waters so much that both the police and the mob will have to accept the scenario we leave behind."

"Oh, right. Well, not to worry. Tom will take care of that. I have every confidence in the dear boy."

Judging by her flush, I suspected she was auditioning another "protégé." I wished I shared her confidence. Tom worried me. He was at the end of his tether, dangerous at this point in the operation, when keeping his two masters happy had never been more crucial. Luca seemed frantic. Tom reported that he kept barking orders and making Tom chase down every rumor in search of his diamonds. Poor Tom also had to find the man we needed and squeeze him just enough so he'd accept a deal—then he had to sell the Bureau on it.

I kept telling myself there was nothing to worry about. That having held on this long, Tom wouldn't quit now. But when he still hadn't shown up at Mother's house more than two hours after he said he would, I figured he had fallen off the tightrope. While debating whether we should make ourselves scarce, I heard a soft knock on the door.

"Where were you?" Mother roared with uncharacteristic vengeance when Tom entered.

Her anxiety probably had less to do with Tom's delay than the fact that Dad had called again while we waited. The lies seemed to come easily enough to her—she calls that acting—but Dad's return had been bumped up to the day after tomorrow. Now we had no margin for error. If Tom failed to finish his part of the operation tonight, we'd never make it.

"Tom…?" I asked tentatively.

"It took longer than I thought, okay? But everything's set. With a little luck, we'll pull it off."

I would have felt better if he hadn't looked like a man who left all his luck behind him.

Tom remembered to leave a message for Luca. "Yo, Antonio," he said, assuming his thug persona for the last time. "I found Paolo. He just had mechanical trouble in that van Martha Collins gave him. Him and me are gonna stop at your old warehouse, where he hid the...merchandise, and we'll see you for breakfast."

I hot-wired the van again, and we drove Paolo through the darkened streets of that abandoned warehouse district in search of Luca's building. Since Tom cradled on his lap the device he had picked up tonight, Mother unlocked the door and lit the light bulb hanging from the ceiling. I drove the van in.

Tom's hands shook so badly he couldn't connect the wires as he'd been instructed to. I moved him aside. I raised my face for one last look at him, longing for some assurance that Luca hadn't turned him. But Tom was already backing toward the door.

I brought the wires together.

My heart stopped.

Despite the eerie silence, I didn't hear the click that Tom said I would when the connection was made. No time to try it again. I sprinted out the door, at what must have been world-record pace, to the place where Tom had taken refuge and was now trying to convince Mother to sacrifice the knees of her hose.

I threw her to the ground and covered her body with my own, and held her there, squirming, while thunder ripped through earth and sky, till the last fragments of metal and mortar and flesh and bone rained down on us.

"Police still have no leads on the van that exploded in the warehouse district yesterday," the news anchor reported. "Not enough remains of the bodies for formal identification, but the two victims are believed to be Paolo Luca and Thomas Ricci, reputed gangland figures. The men were reportedly carrying a small shipment of uncut diamonds."

Mother and I watched the news in a VIP lounge at the airport, while we waited for Dad's plane.

"In a related story, a man identified as Dennis Luca, son of reputed underworld kingpin Antonio Luca, was found dead this morning of execution-style gunshots. Mr. Luca's role in the killing is under investigation."

Mr. Luca's role made me sick. I remembered staking out Folio's. We had to make sure the message we'd sent reached Luca. I wasn't certain whether I'd know on sight after having blown it with Denny. But there was no question. When Luca left the restaurant, his Continental charm had evaporated, leaving a bitter old man. A man who, when faced with the most critical decision of his life, elected to be a businessman, not a father.

Seeing him, and understanding that he'd condemned his own son to death, I knew that despite my protestations, I never really wanted to be anyone else's daughter. I felt a little misty suddenly, and I wanted to hug Mother. But why was she shaking her head?

"Sloppy, Tracy," she said. "Such a poor plan. What were you thinking?"

"Excuse me?"

"Admit it, darling, luck played the primary role. You couldn't be sure the bomb-builder would tell Antonio that it was *Denny* who commissioned the bomb. Nor could you count on it working so well, the police wouldn't guess there had been only one body in the van and would have to rely on Tom's telephone message to make the identification."

That wasn't luck, it was Tom's final arrangement with the Bureau. He delivered Luca on a murder charge, and they leaned on the police to make the identification quickly. Now Tom was safe somewhere in the loving arms of his family with enough of a nest egg to keep their ship from running aground, once they found a fence. Exactly as I planned. My only regret was doubting him.

"And your moral judgment—really, darling. You let criminals settle the score. Is that what you call justice?"

I felt my blood pressure rising. "Come on, Mother, this is L.A. You know the wheels of justice grind chunky-style here. How many trials have we seen where obviously guilty defendants not only got off, but the jury practically threw them a testimonial dinner? This way Denny got the verdict he deserved."

"Well, all I can say is, I hope your father never learns of it. He'd be so disappointed."

So that was what this was about. She should have trusted me more. I had my own secret, didn't I? Fortunately, Drew wasn't expected for another couple of days. Plenty of time for the dust to settle so I could sweep it under the rug.

"Tracy, why are you always so out of step with conventional society?"

I just shook my head. But if you find that question equally perplexing, I suggest you catch a glimpse of Mother at next year's Academy Awards. Take special note of the baubles. Rocks as big as your eyeballs.

Why, indeed.

KRIS NERI has written short mystery fiction for *The Red Herring Mystery Magazine, Mystery Time, Whispering Willow's Mystery Magazine, Woman's World* and many other publications. She is the president of the L.A. Chapter of Sisters in Crime and an active member of Mystery Writers of America. She currently teaches mystery writing at Learning Tree University in Chatsworth, CA.

Angel of Mercy

Marion Rosen

George Nolan was not an ordinary nurse. He breezed through his routine duties in half the time it took the other nurses, but he never took advantage. Even after all the temperatures had been taken and all the medications had been issued, he would never sneak into the nurses' lounge to catch a quick nap or watch TV. No, he truly believed he had a calling. Pure and simple: George Nolan had been placed on this earth to ease pain and suffering.

"How are you this evening, Mrs. McAllister?" George asked the frail, birdlike woman in 47-B.

"I think I'm improving, at least a little," Mrs. McAllister said weakly. "Is it time for my sleeping pill?"

"I just came on duty. Medication will be the next round. Can I get you anything?"

"Yes. A stronger sleeping pill. I don't know why I can't sleep in this place."

Poor thing, George thought as he searched her sinewy wrist for a pulse. *She's slipping through our fingers. A coronary, even a mild one, can be extremely hard on someone her age. Her eyes have disappeared into black, hollow sockets; she's nothing but skin and bones, yet* she *thinks she's improving. It won't be long now, my dear.*

George plumped Mrs. McAllister's pillow, then moved to bed 47-A. Mrs. Harriet Martin was written on the chart, but George saw only a woman who needed to be released from her suffering. She was dying much too slowly, and her agony tortured him. Tonight, he would liberate her, give her the peace he knew she longed for.

By one A.M., the ward was quiet; the only sound was the occasional scrunch of sponge-rubber soles against freshly mopped vinyl. George slipped into the medication room and unlocked cabinet three. Ending Mrs. Martin's torment was the least he could do. It was so easy, he wondered why the other nurses never took it upon themselves to do likewise.

He filled a syringe with potassium chloride and placed it on his medication tray. A heavy dose caused no extreme pain; the drug simply destabilized the patient's heart rhythm. Cardiac arrest was inevitable, especially for someone who had already suffered a heart attack like poor old Mrs. Martin. He felt a surge of satisfaction about the mercy he'd planned for her. She would be at peace long before the morning-shift nurse had plugged in a fresh pot of coffee.

The halls were empty. Thank God, it had been a calm night. George walked by the central station. No call lights were flashing. He continued down the corridor. Two orderlies sat in the nurses' lounge discussing their real or imagined sexual exploits. He hurried by and proceeded to Room 47.

He didn't skip the alcohol wipe before the injection. That would be unprofessional. He eased the fluid into her vein, then pulled the sheet up over her arm.

"Mr. Nolan, what time is it?"

George spun around. "Mrs. McAllister, why aren't you asleep? It's after one in the morning."

Mrs. McAllister's watery old eyes glistened in the dim light. "I've been telling you, those sleeping pills don't work. What's wrong with Harriet? What did you give her?"

"Just her regular medication."

"Isn't there something, a shot maybe, that would help me to sleep?" Mrs. McAllister asked. "Those pills don't work."

"No, not without doctor's orders." He patted her hand. "Try counting sheep."

He closed the curtain that separated the two beds about halfway, then turned off the light. Mrs. McAllister had seen enough for one night.

George waited until almost five before he returned to Room 47. Mrs. McAllister was snoring gently. *Good,* he thought. He pulled back the curtain revealing a very still Mrs. Martin. He checked her pulse. Nothing. She was finally in a happier place than County General.

He followed hospital procedure and hit the code blue button to summon the doctor on duty and all available nursing personnel. He knew it was too late, of course, but he had to give them the chance to display the heroics that would say to the world they had done all they could. George was really the only one who ever took that phrase literally. He never shirked from doing what was necessary to usher these poor dying souls out of their misery.

George stayed close to Dr. Westley as he tried to resuscitate Mrs. Martin. George never missed a cue. He knew what the doctor wanted almost before the doctor knew himself. That's what made a good nurse.

Dr. Westley shook his head. "I thought she was going to make it. Just yesterday, I told her family she was out of the woods."

"That's too bad," George said sympathetically, "but now that nice son of hers and his wife can get on with their lives. Her son told me he was anxious to take a new job in Atlanta, but he didn't want to make the move with his mother still in the hospital."

"Well, he can make the move now, I suppose."

After the doctor left, George began to clean the area, removing all traces of Mrs. Martin into properly coded plastic bags. Her son might want to keep her get-well cards; those went into bag F.

"Nolan?" Dr. Westley stuck his head back into 47-A.

"Yes, Doctor," George answered.

"Thanks for all your help. Sorry you went into overtime. Seems this happens to you a lot, doesn't it?"

"All part of working nights."

"I hate to ask, but since you're still here—"

"Yes, Doctor?"

"There's going to be an inquiry in the chief's office starting today. They'll be posting the notice this morning. Perhaps you could make your statement before you leave. It'll save you a trip in on your day off."

George stiffened. "An inquiry about what?"

"Oh, you know, the statistics game. Whenever there's a disproportionate number of deaths from one thing or another in a certain wing or on a certain shift, they have to check it out. Never leads anywhere, but it gives the pencil-pushers something to do."

"This particular inquiry refers to the night shift?" George asked.

"Yeah, we've lost too many lately. The stats have had an upswing in the last fifteen months."

"Doctor, doctor," a squeaky voice cried from behind the curtain.

George had almost forgotten about Mrs. McAllister. He whipped the curtain from around her bed, slapping it against the wall. She was shrunken and pale, but she sure could yell.

"What's been going on in here?" she demanded.

Dr. Westley stepped to the side of her bed and took her hand. "I'm afraid it wasn't a good night for Mrs. Martin."

"You wheeled her out, didn't you?" She sat up partway, then noticed the bed had been stripped. Her eyes widened. "She died?"

"Yes, I'm afraid so," the doctor answered.

"When can I go home? I don't want to stay in this dreadful hospital another day. I feel just fine."

"Soon. A day or two longer, just to make certain your condition remains stable."

George went to the chief's office that morning. A clerk wrote down everything he said in shorthand, the same way another clerk had taken notes at the inquiry at St. Stephen's a year and a half ago. It seemed like only yesterday. They couldn't file a complaint against him or anyone else, of course. Potassium chloride left no trace. There would be no evidence to support any malpractice, wrongdoing or even negligence. Night staffers couldn't help it that sick people had a tendency to die in their sleep, could they?

George had a hard time sleeping that day, so his step was not quite as bouncy when he returned to the hospital for his shift that night. He'd spent most of the afternoon thinking about moving on again. This time he would go to a warmer state, maybe California; but first he had to take care of a little complication gnawing at the back of his mind. Mrs. McAllister. For someone so sick, she talked a bit too much.

His rounds went quickly. He checked pulses, blood pressures and temperatures, then returned to deliver the evening sleeping pills. One of the other nurses on the floor had called in sick, but that was never a problem for George. He could do the work of three nurses. He was good and he knew it.

He prepared a syringe for Mrs. McAllister and headed for Room 47. No one had been moved to bed A, a lucky break. He switched on the bathroom light, which wasn't bright enough to wake her; but she bolted to her elbows the moment he crept into the shadows just the same.

George placed his medication tray on the bedside table and swabbed her right forearm with alcohol. He noticed her sleeping pill next to the phone.

Her eyes were fixed on the syringe. "I know you gave Harriet something," she whispered. "I know it."

"Now, now, Mrs. McAllister," he soothed. "You forgot to take your sleeping pill. You need your sleep if you want to get well."

She reached out with her other hand and hurled the water thermos against the wall. George scrambled to recover the clanking thermos and then remembered the call button. He yanked the black cord out of her reach, but she wasn't grasping for the button. She plunged the hypodermic needle squarely into his upper arm.

By breakfast, the floor was buzzing with the dreadful news about poor George Nolan. Such a young man to just drop over like that.

Mrs. McAllister rearranged the roses in the vase next to her bed. Down among the stems, the empty syringe was hidden beneath a layer of ferns. When her husband came to visit, she would ask him to take the flowers home. She wanted her lovely roses waiting there to greet her when she checked out of the hospital bright and early the next morning.

MARION ROSEN has two mysteries in print, *Death by Education* and *Don't Speak to Strangers*. She taught English and creative writing for several years while pursuing her own writing projects. Her manuscript, *The Undertaker,* was optioned by Saban Entertainment, and she is currently at work on a new novel, *Death on Delivery*. She is a board member of the Southern California Chapter of Mystery Writers of America.

House of Dreams

Paulette Mouchet

Trevor Cunningham studied the five letters laid evenly side by side on his brother's veneered desk top. Words cut from magazines and newspapers formed a one-sided conversation from the sender. The first, received six weeks ago, read simply:

I am Charlie.

Trevor exhaled softly, the only outward sign of his inner turmoil. As a personal security specialist, he'd seen all kinds of threats, none so elegant in its simplicity. The note, with its double meaning, would say much to a Vietnam vet like his brother, Leo.

The last one read:

Because you have everything.
I have only shattered dreams.

"You show these to the police?" Trevor asked, keeping his tone noncommittal.

Leo, wearing a bright blue-and-white "Cunningham for Congress" button, stubbed out his cigarette in a smokeless ashtray, then spritzed twice with breath freshener. "Nope. I called you, little brother. You're the best there is." Leo grinned at him.

"Which one of us are you trying to convince?" The Stockton fiasco had blown Trevor's reputation to hell and bankrupted PSI, the security company he'd built with his own blood and sweat.

He'd lost his wife and every dime he owned trying to save them and turned to booze when he failed.

Leo looked hurt. "The past is past, little brother. This is blood we're talking about. It's time we were brothers again."

Trevor swallowed another retort. Had Leo *finally* decided to forgive him for bedding his fiancée while he was in country? Karen had come to Trevor looking, he supposed, for a way to be close to Leo while he was gone. Trevor had obliged, though more than once she'd cried out Leo's name in the heat of their passion. "What about your wife?"

"If she had to screw someone, at least we kept it in the family." Leo winked. "Anyway, that was twenty years ago. Karen swears there's nothing between you two." He pushed back his chair. "Want a drink?"

Trevor swallowed hard at Leo's crude offer—a reflection of the bastard his brother had become—and shook his head. He'd been sober eighty-nine days now, thanks to Karen. She dragged him from the gutter, took him to his first AA meeting and gave him the courage to go back when he fell off the wagon.

Leo made his way to the bar, limping only slightly, and mixed a Bloody Mary. "I'm giving you a chance to prove the assholes wrong about you, little brother."

Trevor wondered, *Why now?* When his life collapsed after Stockton, he'd asked Leo for help, but Leo was too busy kissing babies on the campaign trail to bother. And now his war-scarred brother wanted to give him a second chance? Hard to believe, since until today, Leo's opinion of him could have frozen hell.

It hadn't always been that way. In fact, PSI was supposed to have been a joint venture—a business the teenage brothers dreamed of building together after high school—until Leo stepped on a land mine that shattered his leg. Trevor went ahead without Leo, became a personal security specialist and built PSI by himself. Leo went to work for Senator Jack Morgan. They became friends, and it was Morgan who launched Leo's political career using Leo's war injury to woo the pro-military swing vote. Although

Trevor had been banished to the sidelines, he was proud of Leo.

He watched Leo sip his drink and decided he could forgive his brother for offering him one. This might be the only chance they had to put things right again. He tapped the letters. "Who knows about these besides you?"

"This mean you're in?"

"Maybe."

Leo grinned. "Le Marsh, my secretary, knows. And de Franco, my PR man. He's going for a media angle with them."

"Anyone else?"

"Jack Morgan."

Trevor remained neutral, refusing to let his opinion of Senator Morgan ruin this opportunity to make amends with Leo. "Any incidents besides the letters?"

"Yeah. Couple days ago. Le Marsh came back from lunch and the bastard had left a decomposed cat in the office. Jesus, it stunk." Leo settled back in his chair.

"You think the letters and the cat are related?"

"Of course."

"Why?"

"That's your job to figure out, little brother. Uncle Sam sent me to Nam, remember? Five pounds of steel in my leg screwed me out of your career. But that's in the past." Leo smiled his candidate's smile. "Bottom line is, some nut out there wants me dead, and I want you to stop him."

"A dead cat and some weird letters don't add up to murder."

"Someone took a couple shots at me."

Trevor's stomach began to churn. "Where? Any witnesses?"

"No." Leo chuckled, finished his drink and lit up another cigarette. "It was a drive-by while I was taking my morning walk."

"You always take the same route?"

"Right down Rockingham Drive. Five fucking o'clock in the morning. Kinda ironic, don't you think? I got NRA backing and a goddamn punk takes a shot at a cripple in his underwear."

"You didn't get hit?"

"Naw. I dove behind a Mercedes—"

"You get the license plate?"

"No. Someone was trying to kill me for chrissakes."

Trevor sighed. Burying the hatchet was not going to be easy. "Why didn't you tell me about this up front?"

"Didn't want to spoil things."

"What things? What did the police say?"

"Nothing, yet." Leo grinned. "We're doing a reenactment tomorrow morning. Ought to get me five points on my opponent. When de Franco 'leaked' my last death threat, I got three points on the free publicity. Is this fucking America or what?"

"I'm out." Trevor shoved back his chair.

Leo's jaw dropped. "You can't be serious."

"You're more interested in your image than your life."

"That's what politics is all about, little brother."

"But we're talking your *life* here."

"You're right," Leo agreed. "I didn't survive Nam to let some punk plug me two months before I win the election." He stubbed out the second cigarette and spritzed again. "I need you, little brother," he said softly. "Please?"

***

Pam Le Marsh was searching through the piles on her desk for Leo's luncheon speech and trying not to panic, when Karen Cunningham breezed in. Karen wore the mantle of a politician's wife well. A bastion of strength behind Leo, she could run for office herself and win.

"Looking for this?" Karen held out the errant speech.

"Thank God!" Pam exclaimed. "I thought I'd lost my marbles."

"What marbles?" Leo hollered from the hallway.

Pam ground her teeth.

Leo limped in, pushing the stranger into her office. Leo's brows shot up when he saw his wife, hers went up when she saw the stranger, and his went up when he saw her.

Like a bunch of caterpillars mating, Pam thought.

"Well, Trevor—" Karen kissed the stranger on both cheeks.

"How nice to see you."

Leo squirmed, and Pam thought she saw a flicker of jealousy behind his plastic smile.

"You look great," Trevor said with obvious affection.

Who was this Trevor guy, anyway? Pam wondered.

"And you," Karen replied. "I'm glad Leo decided to call you. As you know, he can be very stubborn—"

"Yeah, yeah," Leo interrupted. "What are you doing here, anyway?"

The phone jangled at Pam's elbow.

"Your speech." Karen waved the pages in his direction. "You left it on the kitchen table this morning."

Leo cleared his throat and mumbled something that sounded like "thanks." Karen smiled and kissed him on the cheek, which he maneuvered into an R-rated scene.

Staking out his claim, Pam thought. She shook her head and answered the phone.

"Why the hell hasn't he returned my phone calls?"

She stifled a groan. "He's unavailable, Sen—"

"Bullshit!" the senator roared. "I assume you have some brains in addition to the tits and—"

"Just a moment." She jabbed the button and silently cursed him. When she looked up, she found Trevor staring at her. He certainly hadn't looked at Karen the way he was looking at her. If Leo paid any attention, he'd know his marriage was safe.

"Well?" Leo prompted.

"Senator Morgan," she replied. "He wants your answer about the national health care referendum."

"By God," Leo boomed. "We live in the land of opportunity. A land where a healthy man can get ahead by his wits alone. How *can* we ignore health care?"

The guy was so full of it, she had to remind herself why she didn't quit her job. Working for Leo gave her an insider's view to politics that she wove into her books.

"Put the senator through to my office." Leo headed for the

door. "And by the way," he flicked his wrist toward Trevor, "this is my brother."

Brother? Good thing she was sitting down.

"Whatever he needs," Leo called over his shoulder, "is top priority."

She must have been rattled because she lost the senator when transferring him. Trevor pulled up a chair across from her desk and interrupted her glee. "You don't think much of Senator Morgan," he said.

His face and voice were neutral. Was he baiting her? "He's Leo's biggest campaign supporter. They've been friends for years."

"But he's an ass."

"Are you here to get me fired, or is there another reason?"

Trevor's eyes twinkled.

She crossed her arms and waited.

"Leo hired me to make sure he's still breathing come election day."

"He tell you about the cat?"

"And the Mercedes."

"What Mercedes?"

"A Mercedes took a bullet for him. You can catch it live tomorrow when Leo does the reenactment."

Moron. She shook her head. "Are you two really brothers?"

"According to the birth certificates."

"You have doubts?"

"Let's just say that Leo and I are two *very* different people."

***

Trevor hired Dave Burns, a former PSI employee, for additional security; had Leo's threat letters sent to the FBI lab in D.C. for analysis; and ran background checks on Leo's associates (paying particular attention to Pam Le Marsh).

Pam was determined, and Trevor liked that about her. Anyone who wrote books on the side had to be persistent, and her second novel, a political thriller, was about to hit the market. Pam was pretty, smart, and laughed at his jokes, too. So, when the FBI prelim on the letters came in, Trevor asked her to accompany him to the Bureau, and sent Dave Burns to guard Leo at his meeting with Jack Morgan and the gay rights PAC.

"You should have your keys in hand," he suggested to Pam as the elevators opened onto the parking garage. "If you see something after the elevator leaves, pull the fire alarm. And start screaming."

"For God's sake, Trevor." Pam put her hands on her hips. "It's Leo they're after, not me."

"You *can* scream, can't you?"

"Like this?" She let rip an ear-piercing shriek that reverberated through the parking structure. He winced, slapped his hand over her mouth. She promptly bit his middle finger. He jumped back and grabbed his bleeding digit, more surprised than hurt.

"I think," she sidled up to him with an impish smile, "this is when I kick the guy in the balls to finish him off?"

He stepped back quickly, half-worried she'd really do it.

She eyed his finger, noticed the blood. Her cheeks flushed pink.

He gathered the shreds of his ego. "Should I get out the cross and mirror?"

"I can't believe I did that."

He tipped up her chin and stared into her eyes—earth-colored with a hint of pea green, like his own. "You did the right thing."

"I *bit* you."

"Uh huh." The warmth of her body filled the space between them and made his blood rush. For a moment, the thought of making love to her eclipsed everything else—Leo, the job, *Stockton*— The memory slipped into his fantasy like an ice pick between the ribs. Goddammit! He sucked in a breath and pulled away. He couldn't afford to screw up again.

***

Special Agent Adam Short met Trevor and Pam at the FBI reception desk and escorted them to his office overlooking Westwood. Shorty had deep grooves radiating from the corners of his eyes caused by his habit of blinking every second word. "According to the report"—he blinked—"the guy used gloves. However," he pointed to the third threat sheathed in plastic, "this is an unusual type style. Headquarters is still checking it out, but if we're lucky, it'll be from *Spelunker's Guide to Los Angeles,* with a circulation of two."

Pam picked up the last threat letter. "This font looks like it's from the masthead of *Money* magazine," she offered. "We have a subscription at the office."

Shorty blinked several times, then gave her a placating smile. "Over thirty-one publications use that typeface, ma'am. We're trying to narrow the field *down*." Trevor felt, rather than saw, Pam's irritation.

"All the letters came from the same person," Shorty continued. "You're dealing with a male, mid-to-late forties. And from the use of the word 'Charlie,' he's a Vietnam vet."

"The guy's a psychopath," Pam murmured.

"Who reads *Money* magazine," Trevor added. Shorty glared, but before he could retort, Trevor's cellular phone rang. The hairs on the back of Trevor's neck prickled as he answered.

"The office building has been bombed," Dave Burns announced. "Three people are dead—"

Trevor's soul twisted and he began to shake. *How could he have failed again?* The past erupted from the pit where he'd locked it, vomited up like rotten meat. He licked his lips, hungered for the dulling blanket of oblivion that only a bottle of bourbon could provide. The craving mushroomed like an A-bomb, until it blotted out the fog and everything inside—

"Snap out of it!" Dave yelled in his ear. "Leo's fine! You hear me? He's fine!"

***

Trevor knocked back his third bourbon and set the glass down with a thunk that made Pam jump. She hated to see him like this. Ever since Dave's phone call, Trevor had been oozing with an internal rage she didn't understand. When he had suggested dinner, she agreed, hoping to find words to ease his anger, but he'd driven to a cowboy bar in Malibu instead of a restaurant.

"I'm a drunk." He laughed. "A goddamn drunk."

"Only because you're afraid to face yourself."

He brushed her off with a crude gesture.

"You're a good man, Trevor. Whatever's eating at you isn't worth this." She pointed at his glass.

"Three people died today—"

"That's not your fault. You weren't even at the building."

His eyes smoldered. He waved the barmaid over and ordered another bourbon. "You don't understand."

She folded her arms across her chest. "Try me."

"'Try me,' she says," he sneered into his glass. "What the hell does she know?" He looked up, eyes turning cold and glassy. "Well, 'try this,' lady. I got my fucking partner killed on my last job."

She didn't blink, didn't unfold her arms. "How?"

His lips twitched. "Doesn't matter," he growled.

"Does, too," she shot back. "For all I know you tripped over your own big feet while the guy was in the toilet."

"I knew you wouldn't understand."

"The hell I don't. How do you think NASA felt when the Challenger blew up? Yeah, they screwed up. But they didn't roll over. You think because some people died today that you failed. You should be congratulating yourself for keeping Leo alive, instead of drowning the past in bourbon."

The barmaid brought his drink. Trevor lifted the glass.

"You're doing exactly what the nut wants," she said. "It'll be a lot easier for him to kill Leo if you go around the bend with a bottle."

Trevor considered for a long while—so long, Pam wondered if he'd succumbed to the spurious security of the bar and his drink. Slowly, the anguish that clouded his face dissipated. He took a deep breath, scowled at the liquid in his glass, then set it down, untouched. "It was a fund-raiser in Stockton, Morgan's hometown. The organizers hired me—my company, PSI—to provide security. Leo was there. And, of course, our good friend Senator Jackass Morgan.

"Morgan was at the podium, and I was in the wings, standing next to Leo. We didn't talk, you know. I just happened to be standing next to him. Anyway, there I was, when I spotted a guy with a semi-automatic. Leo saw him at the same time, and we both reacted. I should have figured Leo would do something. I should have remembered about his leg. But I didn't. Leo caught his toe on the carpet, tripped and dumped me on my ass. World-class bodyguard on his fucking ass! The suspect fired at Morgan. My partner materialized from somewhere, dove in front of Morgan and took the bullet between his vest and his armpit.

"Morgan threw a holy temper tantrum. My partner was bleeding to death on the stage and there was Morgan screaming about what an incompetent I was. Christ, they probably heard him in 'Frisco. Never mind that we saved his ass, he said I never should have let the suspect into the fund-raiser in the first place. Morgan filed a lawsuit against me and drove PSI into bankruptcy.

Trevor's face twisted. "I screwed up," he whispered, staring into his drink, "and a good man died."

Pam reached for his hand, cupping his weathered knuckles in her palm.

"I'm afraid—" he choked. "I can't let Leo—my brother—down."

"You won't." She squeezed his hand. "I'm sure."

***

Trevor wrestled open a file drawer and extracted some papers. The cabinet hadn't been the same since the bombing. De Franco milked the media attention for all he could. He got some bleeding heart to donate new office space in Universal City, and they were back in business the next day. Flowers, letters of sympathy and donations—lots of donations—poured in. Leo gained three points on his opponent and basked in the attention.

Pam floated into Trevor's office wearing a clingy yellow blouse and dazzling smile that reminded him of daffodils on a spring day. He'd been sober twenty days now. And for the first time, he *knew* he'd finally put the bottle behind him. She settled into the scarred chair opposite his desk. "You wanted to see me?"

He stared at her, soaking in the way the light played on her hair, the way her earrings sparkled. They'd both been so busy since the bombing, he hadn't seen much of her. "How about dinner tonight?"

She lifted an eyebrow. "Will it be served on a plate?"

He grinned, couldn't possibly be mad at her. "I was thinking the Grand Ballroom of the Beverly Hilton Hotel."

She looked momentarily pleased, then scowled. "Leo's got a black-tie there tonight."

He nodded. "I need a date so I don't stick out like a—"

"You've got balls, Cunningham! I'm not a piece of fluff for you to wave at the media." She looked like she might pop him.

"Absolutely not," he agreed soberly. "I have to fill the empty chair next to me, and, well, I hoped you'd be in it." He gave her a Charlie Brown look, dripping with sincerity.

"Damn you." She exhaled, waggled a finger at him. "Nothing had better happen."

"We'll see," he said, hoping with all his heart that something *did* happen afterwards. "If it makes you feel any better, I hired a third man for backup. His name is Sutton, Bill Sutton."

***

From the head table, Trevor studied the ballroom as the waiter cleared their dinner plates. Dishes clattered. The band played "Yankee Doodle Dandy." The crowd hummed with privileged excitement. Sixty-three tables of eight people each—five hundred guests—had coughed up the thousand-dollar-a-plate donation for the opportunity to rub elbows with candidate Leo Cunningham and his pal, Senator Jack Morgan. Many wore red ribbons showing their support for AIDS victims. Most sported the special-edition campaign buttons that de Franco's people gave out at the door. All were potential killers.

At his elbow, Pam sipped a seltzer and followed his gaze around the room. Leo spritzed with breath freshener, then smiled at the crowd. Morgan, sitting next to Karen, fiddled with his unused wine glass and looked vaguely uncomfortable. As far as Trevor knew, Morgan had remained sober at only one other fund-raiser.

Bill Sutton's soft voice in his earphone assured Trevor the kitchen aisles were clear and the two rear exits were secure. Trevor checked his watch and told Bill to stay in the kitchen. A few seconds later, Dave Burns reported an all-clear for the hotel lobby and the main ballroom exits.

"So," Senator Morgan looked up, as if an intelligent thought had occurred to him, and gave Trevor a predatory grin. "You still think you have what it takes to keep anybody alive?"

Trevor pretended not to hear.

"I would have thought," Morgan continued, "after you screwed up your last job, you'd have gotten smart. Gone into real estate." He turned to Leo. "Real nice of you to give your brother a second chance. Forgive and forget. That's the American way." He took in the crowd with a sweep of his arm as the last of the dinner plates disappeared through the kitchen double doors. "That's why we're all here for ya, Leo. That's why—"

"Give it a rest," Pam snapped. "Trevor's doing a fine job."

Morgan snapped his lips into a lethal line. "You bitch! This asinine ad for steroids," he pointed at Trevor, "about got me killed."

Her eyes flashed. "Yeah, and his partner took the bullet."

"That's enough!" Leo slammed his fist on the table. The entire ballroom conversation came to a screeching halt as five hundred pairs of eyes riveted on the head table. "You're fired, Le Marsh! You hear me? Fired!"

"Fine!" Pam glared at him, tossed her napkin on the table and marched out.

Trevor watched her leave, desperately wanting to go after her. Leo sat down, smiled at the crowd as if nothing had happened. The band struck up a lively tune, and the ballroom returned to normal. A few seconds later, the lights dimmed abruptly. Trevor's pulse shot up. The band lurched into the national anthem, the kitchen double doors swung open, and waiters began to parade out. Each wore an Uncle Sam top hat and carried a tray of flaming Baked Alaska. It looked like the Fourth of July. The crowd "oohed" and "ahhed." Leo and Morgan turned their attention to the dessert and began to clap enthusiastically as two waiters approached their table. When they were close enough for Trevor to see individual desserts on the trays, one waiter lifted a napkin from the center of his tray, exposing a weapon. Trevor didn't think. He didn't wonder if alcoholism had dulled his edge, or if failure had robbed him of his nerve. He acted.

As the gunman tossed the tray, Trevor leaped to his feet with the instinct and confidence of a well-trained bodyguard. Two shots slammed into his Kevlar vest as he jumped in front of Leo, knocking them both to the floor. Leo yelped. Pain girdled Trevor's chest and sucked the air from his lungs. He shook off stars, yanked his weapon from under his jacket and rolled into a sitting position in front of his brother. The gunman turned and dashed for the double doors.

Trevor lurched to his feet barking into his lapel mike, "He's headed for the kitchen. Five feet eight, in waiter's garb."

The gunman fired two wild shots at him. People screamed. Baked Alaska tumbled. Dave Burns crashed through the ballroom's main doors, weapon drawn. "Take care of Leo!" Trevor bellowed.

The gunman bolted into the kitchen, grabbed a junior chef by the throat and put the gun to his head. "Back off," the gunman growled at Trevor.

"Let the kid go," Trevor said evenly.

The gunman assessed Trevor's restraint and laughed. "Go ahead, asshole."

Trevor eyed the gunman, then shrugged. "Some days you win and—"

Bill Sutton fired twice from behind a pallet of lettuce. The gunman stumbled—gaping with surprise as two bullets slammed into his right shoulder. Bright red spattered the shiny, stainless steel counters. The junior chef twisted away and dove behind an institutional Kitchen Aid. Trevor's finger twitched four times on the trigger of his weapon, and the gunman keeled over dead.

From Baked Alaska to Forest Lawn—in less than three minutes. Trevor let out his breath.

He'd wiped the slate clean.

Trevor left Bill Sutton to deal with the body and headed to the ballroom. Dave Burns was doing his best to hold back the press, but Morgan and Leo, with Karen solidly at his side, were milking the attention for all they could. Morgan touched off a media stampede when he spotted Trevor and hollered, "That's the man I was telling you about!"

Reporters fired questions at Trevor like Serb artillery. One voice—belonging to a CNN correspondent—rose above the din: "Why has your security team twice failed to prevent an assassin from breaking in?"

He suddenly felt tired, felt the ache of cracked ribs where the bullets struck his vest.

"Was this suspect working with the first one?" the CNN reporter pressed.

Trevor sighed. The man's questions were reasonable, he decided. The answers, however, eluded him.

***

The next day, Leo told Trevor that although he was pleased with Trevor's performance, public opinion went the other way, and, after much consideration, he and Jack Morgan felt it was best to let Trevor go. "Image, little brother," Leo said with his candidate's smile. "With the race so close, I can't have an albatross like this hanging around my neck, you understand."

Trevor packed his bags and went home. For the next two weeks, the *Times* carried the story in some form or another, until Trevor was so sick of the convolutions and lies that he canceled his subscription. He desperately wanted to see Pam, but her publisher had sent her on a book tour, so he made the AA meeting rounds and counted the weeks until her return.

The CNN reporter's questions stuck in Trevor's craw and he spent a lot of time in the back row of smoke-filled rooms mulling things over, while an endless stream of faces talked about their alcoholism. Shorty told him the guns used in both Stockton and Beverly Hills had been reported stolen from a shop in San Francisco; but Trevor didn't begin to piece things together until he misread his AA meeting list and accidentally went to one for gays. Senator Jack Morgan's closest aide was there—unaware of Trevor sitting two rows behind him—bragging about how he'd finessed twenty-three consecutive days of coverage for Morgan's campaign in the *San Francisco Chronicle*. That's when it hit Trevor like the proverbial ton of bricks: Morgan would stop at nothing to obtain a front-page headline. Being the target of one attempted murder and the close friend of the second target had been no accident.

***

Trevor stood to the side and studied the throng of people clustered around the table where Pam was signing books. For the moment, it was enough to just watch her. He'd worried that she didn't want to see him again. That when she marched out of the ballroom, she'd marched out of his life, as well. He cut to the front of the line, held her gaze in his. "I didn't want to let you go."

"I know. You had to stay with Leo." She leaned forward and searched his face. "You okay?"

She wasn't asking about his ribs. "I bought stock in Perrier." He grinned. She smiled back—daffodils again.

"Good for you. Leo was an ass for not sticking by you. Served him right to lose the election." Suddenly, her face went white and she pointed behind him.

Trevor spun, saw a flash of movement from under the coat of a ski-masked man at the rear of the crowd. *"Everybody get down!"* he bellowed, dumping the table toward Pam for cover. Fans scattered like frightened birds. Trevor dove behind a display of best sellers and reached for his weapon as the ski-masked man pumped several rounds in his direction. Trevor rolled, popped up from behind the best sellers and fired twice. The impact blew the masked man backward into a rack of Anne Rice paperbacks. He hovered for a moment, then slid to the floor, leaving a streak of red down several covers of *Interview with the Vampire.*

Trevor approached cautiously as the man struggled for air. Morgan was reelected last night, so what did he have to gain by this? And why shoot Pam? Trevor's gut twisted when he thought of Pam dead. He wrenched the gun from the bastard's hand and pulled off the mask.

"Goddamn," Leo sputtered. "You and the fucking cat. Run 'em over and they come back for more."

Trevor stared, mind spinning as his world disintegrated like Hiroshima.

Pam crawled over, gasped when she recognized Leo.

Trevor clutched her hand like a grounding rod and squeezed back the avalanche of betrayal. "My own brother," he croaked, "was behind Stockton—" Pam held him tightly, as if a puff of wind would blow him away. He stared at Leo, as the picture of what happened came into numbing focus. "You knew Morgan was gay."

"But he's married," Pam said. "Has two kids—"

"Yeah," Leo spat, then winced. "You think California would reelect a faggot?"

"You threatened to go public with it if Morgan didn't help you. Morgan agreed and in the world of spin control saw a way to garner some publicity for himself, as well. He got the weapon and you—" Trevor forced the words, silently begging his brother to rear up and tell him he was full of shit. "—you staged the first shooting." Leo managed a spiteful grin. "The plan worked perfectly until Karen—"

"Always figured," Leo wheezed, "you two were still balling each other."

Trevor shook his head, pushing on like a travel-weary member of the Donner Party. "When Karen got me sober, got my life back on track, she ruined everything. So you devised Plan Two: You created a stalker, mailed yourself some threat letters—"

"Using words cut from *Money* magazine," Pam whispered.

"And hired me to take a bullet at the Beverly Hilton Hotel, which people would assume was meant for you."

Leo's silence consumed the last flicker of Trevor's hope. He grabbed his brother by the collar and shook. "Why, Leo? Goddammit, why?"

"Because, little brother..." A feeble grin. Blood and spit dribbled out of the corner of Leo's mouth. "Because...you had...my dream..."

PAULETTE MOUCHET authored the well-received series *Horse-back Riding Trails of Southern California*. She currently writes a column for *Ride!* magazine. Her work has also appeared in the *Equestrian Trails* magazine, *Country Journal* and *Byline* magazine. Past editor of the SinC/LA newsletter and co-editor of its hit cookbook, *Desserticide aka Desserts Worth Dying For*, she now serves as treasurer of the organization.

Speak No Evil

Gayle McGary

Laurel slapped her hand down on the compact to stop it from clattering as it hit the sink. She held her breath and listened. Her heart thunked and she heard a mockingbird singing in the top of the maple outside the trailer. All the rest was silence. That unnerved her. She took a slow, shallow breath and her eyes jumped to the spot on the mirror where Bud's angry face would appear if the noise woke him up. She heard a cough and the creak of old springs as Bud turned over in bed just a few feet away. The snoring began again, and Laurel let her breath out with a soft sigh. She picked up the silver compact. *You're really up against the wall, Lore.*

She opened the compact and dabbed makeup on the purplish black bruise over her right eye. Her face was now covered with a mask of Avon Honey Beige. But it wasn't going to hide the swelling. She'd be wearing her sunglasses today at work again.

Laurel rubbed her fingers over the cheap aluminum compact embossed with twined roses, now worn smooth. It was precious to her. It had belonged to her mother, and she had played dress-up with it as a child. She dropped it into her makeup bag, straightened her brown uniform and tiptoed out of the bathroom into the living room/kitchen.

The trailer she shared with Bud she had once shared with her mother. It was an old Airstream and the smallest trailer in the park. Bud loved to say, "Jeez Looeez, Lore, your old lady must've thought she was gonna raise a midget in here. It sure ain't big enough for two normal people."

Laurel's shoes crunched as she walked across the mess on the linoleum to get the broom and dustpan. The old portable TV lay on its side on the couch, its gray plastic case cracked. Her collection of glass animals now lay in bright shards on the floor. Like the compact, the animals were a connection to her mother, Rose. She remembered the excitement she felt as a child when her mother presented her with a new one for each birthday. Laurel looked at them with dull eyes. She felt strangely matter-of-fact as she swept them up. *Just a bunch of bygones,* she thought, *little bits of life gone by.*

Bud was forever telling her, "It's history, babe. Get over it." And once he had said, "One more time and *you're* history, babe." She couldn't remember what she had done or had not done to provoke him.

The colored glass animals that had been crushed under Bud's boots now glittered like tiny prisms. She put the TV back on the fold-out table and found one survivor underneath. A little glass monkey, one of a set of three, little Speak No Evil, with his hands clapped over his mouth. She dropped him into her pocket. She knew See No Evil and Hear No Evil were "history."

The night before, Bud rousted her out of bed at midnight. "This shitty trailer. It's closing in on me." His eyes flicked around the small space and lit on Laurel's collection of glass animals. "The goddamn place is small enough without cluttering it up with this goddamn junk." He reached out and backhanded them and the TV in one powerful blow. The TV bounced once and landed on the couch. Bud ground the broken glass bits into the linoleum as he stomped over to her. He hit her in the belly—why did he always go for the gut? She ducked and the second punch hit her in the eye. "Everybody's got to learn a little lesson now and then," said Bud, breathing hard as he pushed past her and fell into bed. She lay awake that night, curled up next to the TV, wondering how she could change her life.

Looking out the window, she drank the rest of her cold coffee. At five-thirty in the morning, the sun was beginning to cast sharp pink rays across the tops of the trailers. Whispering Pines Mobile Home Park was in a hollow of land otherwise plowed and planted with truck crops as far as the eye could see. It was surrounded by a grove of tall, dusty eucalyptuses. There was not a pine tree in sight here in the Central Valley, where Laurel had lived all of her twenty-one years.

Across the lane, Mrs. Tuck and Mr. Hansen were already working in their gardens. Their spouses dead and gone, they treated each other with respect and an affection Laurel had rarely seen between women and men. As she watched, their eyes flicked to her window. She ducked back out of sight. *Well, they'd have to be deaf to have missed the noise last night.*

She pressed gingerly at the swelling over her eye and put on her blue-rimmed sunglasses. Today was Friday and she and Arlene both finished at the restaurant at six o'clock. Since Bud had just come off a four-day run, she could trust him to be out with his buddies tonight. Maybe she could talk Arlene into helping her shop for a new outfit for the office temp interview. She pulled *Gourmet Budget Meals for Two* off the shelf over the sink and riffled the pages. Once, twice. Once more. Slowly. Page by page. It was gone. The money wasn't there. Had she put it in a different book? There were only five others. She pulled them off one by one. The money wasn't there. Bud had found it. Bud had taken it. Sixty bucks she had saved. He'd done it before. "Who makes the real money around here?" he'd yelled as he pocketed it.

Laurel grabbed her bag and slammed out the door. She glanced across the lane on her way to the car. Mrs. Tuck nodded and Mr. Hansen said, "Morning," and they bent back to their work. *They have order in their lives,* she thought. *They have some control. They can plan and make things happen.* She yanked open the car door and threw her bag inside. She gunned the motor as she backed out into the lane. The car stalled.

Bud threw open the trailer door and hopped barefoot across the gravel. He stood bare-chested and beer-bellied, his hands planted on the hood of the car.

"Goddammit, Laurel, I told you I need the goddamn car today. You take the goddamn bus. You move your ass a little, you can goddamn catch it."

As he stood there glaring, Laurel wanted to slam her foot down on the gas and plow right into him. *I could do it!*

Laurel pulled the car back up over the inky blots of oil leaks. Mrs. Tuck and Mr. Hansen pretended not to watch as she got out of the car. Bud went back into the trailer. *What if I'd had the guts to do it?* She walked down the lane toward the highway bus stop.

Big Five Truck Stop was in a complex of gas stations, mini-markets and fast food restaurants off Interstate 5. It was tacked onto a two-story motel where trucks overnighted, their engines running, diesel fumes curling into the air. It was an oasis of transients, people passing through to someplace else. Laurel had worked there since she was sixteen.

Arlene was wiping up the counter in front of a couple of truckers, when she noticed Laurel in sunglasses. "That man's going to kill you one of these days. What're you going to do then?"

The truckers raised their eyebrows, and one of them made a comment Laurel didn't catch. Arlene took their cups away and slapped down their bills. Arlene was barely five feet tall, with pitted skin under heavy makeup. Her lips and fingernails were painted a bright red. She was trim, energetic and a hard worker. She was at least fifteen years older than Laurel, and Laurel thought she was beautiful. She also thought Arlene would never put up with the things she endured.

"You got to watch out for yourself, hon," Arlene said later, on break out back. Arlene smoked a cigarette. "Other people don't watch out for you. They don't want to get involved. It's like when those people get themselves killed in front of a whole crowd who don't do nothing." Her eyes narrowed and she shook her head, her long black hair swaying over her narrow shoulders. "Or some man beats up his wife and kids and the neighbors see everything, hear everything, and never open their mouths to say a word."

Arlene took a deep drag and ground out the butt with her heel. Arlene always had an opinion, but it sounded like she had been saving this one up and wanted to get rid of it.

"And it don't make no difference if a man is the president of some company or just a workingman like your Bud. Some men have just got some hateful meanness locked up in them from when they were kids. Most of the time, they're sweet as candy, but when things hit bottom, you got to watch out. When things go wrong for them, it's you they blame. They can love you like crazy, and that might be part of it, I don't know, but it don't stop them from thinking everything is your fault."

Things hadn't always been this bad with Bud. They had been good at first. Real good. Laurel knew she was attractive to men. She learned how to keep men interested without giving up too much of herself—until the right man came along. She thought that man was Bud. At first, he was just another one of the truckers idling his rig overnight in the motel parking lot next to the restaurant. But he was damn good-looking. He'd played football in high school, "the best time of my life," and at twenty-eight, he was still trim, with just a hint of a belly developing. He made good money. He brought her roses and made her laugh, and soon she found herself staying overnight with him in the motel. He was from Sacramento, but there was "nothing there I can't walk away from." He moved into the trailer with her in Whispering Pines.

The first year, Bud claimed to be settling down. "You might hear some stories about me, babe, but I'm a family man now." It was easy for Laurel to believe it then. He still brought roses. He was on the road four days out of seven and had to catch up on his sleep at the end of a run. But then they would go dancing. Bud loved to dance. "I'm a mover, babe," Bud would say. "It's like football. You got to be a mover." He'd do that little bump-and-grind shimmy like players did after they scored.

Bud came home with a Rottweiler pup. It hadn't seemed to dawn on him how big a Rottweiler was going to become. It seemed to Laurel that they were a family with a future. She got pregnant and kept it a secret, waiting for the right moment to spring the big news.

The pup was gone one night when she came home from work. The little bitch had run away, Bud told her. Didn't appreciate a good home. Laurel drove around the park and out to the highway, but she knew in her heart it was useless. Bud had gotten rid of the dog because it would not come when he called. He yelled at it and beat it with a newspaper, so it would not come to him. The pup came easily to Laurel, butt wiggling, licking her face, trying to climb into her lap. Bud was jealous.

Laurel waited another month before she told Bud she was pregnant. "I just wanted to be sure, honey," she said. One night, he was in a good mood; they were dancing. He picked her up and swung her around and they danced cheek to cheek. Later, they made love, and Laurel thought things were really going right.

When Arlene dropped Laurel off, it was close to seven o'clock. The car was gone. She freshened her makeup and began chopping onions for a meat loaf. She would make a nice dinner. Bud was always hungry. She put the meat in the oven, set the timer and took a sandwich and a Pepsi outside. It was dusk, Laurel's favorite time of day. The light was so pretty and the air felt soft. She put her feet up and leaned back.

There was something new in Mr. Hansen's garden. She shaded her eyes against the low setting sun and squinted at the brown thing next to his cement birdbath. It looked like some kind of animal made out of branches. A little deer. You would never mistake it for a real deer, but it looked so lively. Silhouetted against the setting sun, dust motes shimmering in the rays of yellow light, the deer seemed to move its head and look at her.

Laurel looked at her own "garden": an old weathered picnic table, a couple of Kmart plastic chairs and an old lounge chair.

Things can change. She'd work on the yard this weekend, when she could count on Bud sleeping late. He never got up till after noon.

Laurel rose at her usual quarter to five and stood outside drinking coffee. She watched the deer in Mr. Hansen's garden come alive again. It was just a bunch of sticks, as Bud would probably tell her, but someone had very carefully curved and bundled the branches and bound them with twine into the shape of a life-sized deer. It was very graceful. It reminded Laurel of a camping trip when she was a child. She had slept outside in her sleeping bag and awakened early in the morning and saw a doe and her two little fawns nibbling plants on the slope of the hill in front of her. She lay still, not wanting to scare them. The doe turned and saw her but didn't run away, and Laurel watched them until they disappeared over the rise.

Mrs. Tuck came out into her garden and stood looking at Mr. Hansen's deer. She nodded to Laurel. "It's so cute," Laurel called.

"Oh, isn't it," crowed Mrs. Tuck, like she was just waiting for Laurel to say something. "Can't you just see it walking over to take a drink out of Mr. Hansen's birdbath?" Laurel could. She thought it should have its own little pool. "Mr. Hansen's going to make one for my garden," Mrs. Tuck called out. "Maybe he'll make one for you. We'll have a wild animal park." Mrs. Tuck laughed. Laurel laughed along with her. It felt neighborly, something Bud had always discouraged.

"I hate to see you out there gossiping with those old farts," Bud had said. "They got nothing better to do, but that doesn't mean you don't."

That afternoon, Bud lay on the lounge chair outside, drinking beer and eating chips as he watched TV. Laurel worked on her garden, hauling fieldstones from the drainage ditch at the edge of the park and arranging them in a circle around a little plot of dirt. During commercials, Bud roused himself to tease Laurel, but he reserved most of his sarcasm for Mr. Hansen's "shitty pile of sticks."

He warned her, "Lore, you're not bringing any shitty pile of sticks into *this* yard." Bud had started out in a good mood with a kiss on her neck and a tender squeeze. She didn't know what was annoying him now.

After a while, Bud got bored when he couldn't get a rise out of Laurel and took off in the car. "I'm out of here, babe. Don't expect me for dinner." That was fine with Laurel. She had plans.

That night, Laurel dug through the boxes in the closet, finding what she was looking for under a pile of clothes. She pulled it from the box and shook it out, releasing a sharp vinyl smell. A bright spill of primary colors: starfish and shells and seahorses. It was a cheap plastic kid's wading pool from Kmart. Only seven months ago, she had opened this silly little gift from Arlene. Beneath it were layette sets and receiving blankets. Her breath caught in her chest with a sharp pain.

She ran her hands over the plastic, feeling for cracks, wondering if it would still hold water. She found the hand pump Bud used to inflate his football and started to pump. It would go a lot faster if she borrowed Mr. Hansen's bicycle pump, but he'd probably ask questions or want to do it for her. She didn't want to answer any questions.

It had been on a Saturday night like this one, over ninety degrees all day, and it hadn't cooled off much by evening. Bud was out with the guys. Laurel had planned a special dinner, but Bud said, "It's been a shit week, babe. I got to relax a little." He came home earlier than usual. Laurel was on the lounge chair outside drinking lemonade. She had been running the fan in the trailer, door and windows open, but it was still like an oven inside. Bud got out of the car and walked past her into the trailer. He called out to her.

She remembered it clearly. She went in to pour him a glass of lemonade. He hit her low in her back. Slammed her up against the door. The pitcher hit the floor and lemonade flew in all directions. Later, sitting on the floor waiting for the ambulance, she could only separate the stickiness of the lemonade from the stickiness of the blood by the color.

The pain from the blow was eclipsed by the painful thought: *He killed the baby.* She thought this over and over while Bud threatened, then apologized, and then begged her to forgive him. When she came home from the hospital, Bud was very protective. Laurel felt empty. Since then, there wasn't a day when she didn't think about how fast dreams can die.

The wrinkles in the plastic filled out slowly and the seahorses became plump as the pool inflated. It was smaller than she re-membered. She closed the valve and pushed the pool into the back of the closet, piling boxes in front of it. She would set it up tomorrow morning. Bud didn't come home until midnight. He didn't notice the clutter in the closet. And he left her alone.

Sunday, Laurel was up before dawn. While the coffee perked, she retrieved the wading pool from its hiding place and set it out-side, piling rocks around the sides to hide the plastic and make it look more natural. She filled it with water. She stood back and admired it as the sun rose. Bud couldn't complain about the pool's upkeep. It hadn't cost a penny, so he couldn't complain about money. He even might like it.

That afternoon, she made potato salad, marinated two fat chickens and cleaned out the electric barbecue. Bud came out at one o'clock and told her right away he had a hangover and didn't want any lip; but he circled her waist and nuzzled her neck, so she had every reason to hope for a nice day. Laurel passed the TV out through the window to Bud. He made her go back and find the duct tape and repair the TV's cracked case before he settled down on the lounge chair outside to drink beer and watch the game. The picture was grainier than usual, but Bud was sure it was that satellite dish two lanes over that was sucking off his reception.

Halfway through his second six-pack, Bud started the barbecue.

If he liked anything as much as beer and football, it was firing up the barbecue and burning meat. Bud lit a cigarette and ran skewers through the chickens. His eyes gleamed as he doused the charcoal with lighter fluid, threw in a match and watched the flames whump up.

Later, Laurel couldn't really say how things had escalated. It might have had something to do with the primal power Bud felt behind a blazing fire. Or, it might have been Mrs. Tuck having the gall to bring over a fruit salad, saying she'd made a little too much and it would be a shame to waste it. Maybe it was Mr. Hansen, emboldened by Mrs. Tuck's generosity, seizing his little stick deer under his arm and trotting it across the lane and presenting it to Laurel. Bud turned from the barbecue and leveled the can of lighter fluid like a pistol, drenching the deer. Mr. Hansen dropped it and leapt behind the picnic table. Bud threw his cigarette at the deer and it shot up in a blaze, the dry wood crackling and sparking, flames clearing the top of the trailer. Laurel and Mrs. Tuck darted behind the table and screamed as sparks showered their hair.

"Water!" Mr. Hansen yelled. He ran toward Laurel's pool.

Bud jumped into the pool in front of him, wielding the knife like he was in hand-to-hand combat.

"Are you crazy?" Laurel screamed. She threw a towel over Mrs. Tuck's burning hair and slapped at her own.

Bud slashed at the plastic, gutting yellow starfish and pink seahorses. The blade pinged off the rocks. Water poured from the pool, the fieldstones slowing the flow.

Laurel screamed, "Murderer!"

She picked up the TV and threw it.

At the final moment, Bud dropped the knife, raising his arms to receive the TV. It passed high and wide and plummeted to the rocks behind him. It bounced into the pool. Bud shuddered, his hips shaking, arms still locked high to receive the pass, as his heart took the current.

Later, when the deputy sheriff came, Mrs. Tuck said, "Bud was all set to fix that little pool for Laurel. He was stepping into it and somehow his foot got messed up with the TV. It got dragged into the pool, and he just started jumping. It was a real old TV." She glanced at Mr. Hansen for confirmation. They both looked at Laurel, who sat alone at the picnic table.

"That the way you saw it?" the deputy asked Mr. Hansen. He sounded just like one of those TV cops to Mr. Hansen. Mr. Hansen nodded. The deputy shook his head, and Mr. Hansen thought maybe the deputy didn't believe him. They were both staring at the bloody rocks behind Bud's head. The knife lay in a puddle of water. Mr. Hansen said, "Well, you see, officer, Bud was going to go in and fix the pool with that duct tape he was putting on the cracked TV. That stuff'll fix anything. Fixed my antenna with it just last week." He attempted to direct the deputy's attention across the lane to his trailer, but the deputy's attention was now on the pile of charred wood by their feet. A whole new crime had claimed the deputy's attention.

"You people having unprotected fires out here?"

"No, sir, no, sir," said Mr. Hansen. "That's...that's..."

"That's charcoal for the plants," interrupted Mrs. Tuck. "Does the soil real good."

The deputy made a few notes on his pad and turned his attention to Bud's body, bulky under black plastic, now being loaded into an ambulance. He glanced at Laurel, who seemed in shock, sitting dry-eyed and withdrawn at the picnic table. He'd seen that before. She'd be crying soon enough. "You going to be all right, ma'am? These folks here tell me they're going to stick around if you need some help." He didn't see any reason to stick around himself. He was writing this one up as an accident.

Laurel shook her head. She stared at her pool, tattered now beneath the rock ring, the cracked gray box of the TV set still glistening with water. A little breeze came up and the small puddle of water under the TV quivered as though electrical current still zapped through it.

Laurel felt the first tears slide down her cheeks. She reached into her pocket for a tissue and her fingers closed around something hard. She pulled out the glass monkey, little Speak No Evil, and held it up. The sun winked off its tiny hands clasped tightly over its mouth.

GAYLE McGARY earned an MFA at UCLA in sculpture, painting and graphic arts. She exhibits her artwork nationally and teaches at L.A. City College. She designed the cover art for SinC/LA's *Desserticide.* She is currently writing her first novel, a thriller featuring a woman firefighter. She lives in Altadena with her husband, Richard Partlow, also a writer.

The Shakedown

Kevin Gillogly

For a lot of folks in Boone County, last year was anything but a boon. It was tough enough to endure an economic recession, and even natural calamities, such as tornadoes, floods and blizzards. It was quite another to be left bereft in the wake of Lester Crone.

For Lester, the year proved to be one of exceptional vintage. From the profits of his Mr. Fix-It rogue construction enterprise, he was able to purchase a new truck, a bass boat and a top-of-the-line slate pool table. It also allowed him the luxuries of a satellite dish and a big-screen TV. These last two creature comforts made it easier for him to track his investments while he relaxed in his newly furnished rec room. But it wasn't the stock market he played. Nor were commodity futures a lure. As far as the burly bricklayer knew, a blue chip was something you anted in a poker game. Frozen pork bellies were hunks of meat you pulled from the freezer and tossed on the grill.

No, Lester followed his fortunes religiously every Sunday, sort of his personal day of worship. The enormous amounts of cash pocketed in the spring and summer months were now flowing into the coffers of his bookie, the result of ill-fated, long-shot bets on football games. Each week, Lester placed increasingly large bets in an attempt to recover the previous weeks' losses. As autumn turned to winter, his financial outlook darkened with the fading light of day. By the time the Super Bowl rolled around at the end of January, the only thing Lester could afford to change was his name, and if he were to renew his practice of bilking unsuspecting homeowners, he'd have to.

His method was simple, though not especially original. While cruising the quiet residential streets of the towns throughout the county, Lester looked for homes that were likely to shelter senior citizens. He soon learned that houses displaying the American flag were good tip-offs. Similarly, yards and gardens dotted with lawn ornaments, bird feeders, whirligigs and wind spinners suggested that the owners were likely retirees who had time to devote to such details.

Once noted, the routine was the same. Lester would ring the doorbell and politely inform the lord or lady of the manor that, while performing some remodeling work in the area, he just happened to notice a visible defect in the chimney. Knowing that no one welcomes bad news, he mastered the art of intimation. By suggesting that an unstable chimney collapse could lead to a devastating personal injury lawsuit by a neighbor, guest or even a gas meter reader, he set his trap. For those who balked or raised an eyebrow, Lester was quick to dispatch the ladder from his truck. He would then ascend the chimney spire and effectively simulate a rocking motion that gave the illusion of a precarious condition. This sleight of hand was his pre-closer. He next had to convince the mark that he, Lester Crone, could make the repairs that very day—and for a fraction of what one of those high-priced "Yellow Pages" contractors would charge. By offering to work off the books for cash, he further offered a twenty-percent discount. Between his concerned manner and his ability to get the prospect to envision paying double or triple the amount to another contractor, Lester proved to be a better salesman than he ever was a bricklayer.

At first, he made an effort to deliver some cursory or cosmetic remedy. But after a dozen or so slipshod jobs, he discovered his persuasive abilities alone were often sufficient to exact a cash down payment for the "materials and supplies" needed to commence work. He figured he could make more tax-free cash and work less by merely setting up these quick hits. Leaving the trusting souls nodding, he would drive off in search of his next pigeon. The only thing his customers got out of the deal was a flimsy business card with a fictitious phone number. He worked this way all last year, and he could do it again. Though now, he needed a new identity. He knew if anyone looked into the county's Better Business Bureau, the "Lester Crone/Mr. Fix-It" file would not be filled with letters of glowing praise. But the "Larry Crown/Master Builder" file would be as empty as Lester's current bank account.

The trouble was this: Lester, now Larry, was not only cursed with limited foresight that made him such a poor prognosticator of football games, he was also lean in hindsight. All last year, when his business was rolling along, he never bothered to keep records or note addresses. This now posed a problem. Having canvassed so much territory, what if he now approached a home where he had been before? They wouldn't know Larry Crown. But would they recognize him as Lester Crone? Perhaps, Lester concluded, a disguise might do the trick. At the corner drugstore, he found a cheap pair of nonprescription reading glasses and picked up a Cleveland Browns cap from the bargain bin, for good measure.

Soon he was back on patrol. It didn't take long to locate a house that fit the ideal profile. It was a charming bungalow with colorful gnome figures positioned along the window flower boxes and a fifteen-foot-high brick chimney. Even Old Glory waved to him from a pole mounted to the front porch. Slipping on his new glasses and hat, Lester emerged from the cab and performed a pantomime as he eyed the chimney. He stood there for a few moments, rubbing his chin to create a look of concern, should the dwelling's owner just happen to peer out the window. He then approached the door and dropped the heavy cast iron knocker.

While waiting for an answer, he tugged the bill of his cap and adjusted the fit of his glasses, whose distorted view was already beginning to give him a headache. After a second knock, the door opened as far as its brass security chain would allow. "Who is it?" a meek voice inquired.

"Excuse me, ma'am, I'm Larry Crown, Master Builder. That's my truck over there. As I was driving by your lovely home, I couldn't help but—"

"I didn't call a builder," the voice spoke louder.

"No, you don't understand. Your chimney appears to be in need of repair. I just wanted to alert you of the danger, Mrs... Mrs...?"

"Mrs. Vance. Evelyn Vance," she said while releasing the security chain and revealing herself as the gentle grandmotherly type Lester had hoped for. "You say I'm in danger?"

Bingo, thought Lester. *The hook was set. This would be a quick sale. Better to give her both barrels.* "I just thought you ought to be aware of the consequences. You know, a good stiff wind might topple that chimney. And what with our lawsuit-happy society today, you could lose more than just your chimney. You could lose your home, and maybe even your life's savings." Lester took a beat to let the weight of his words fall squarely where he had intended.

"Are you sure?"

"'Fraid so, Mrs. Vance. Look, I'll show you." Lester trotted off to his truck and hoisted the extension ladder from its rack onto his shoulder. Its lightweight aluminum construction made it easy for him to manage alone. Laying the ladder along the length of the chimney, he began his ascent. Normally, he had no problem negotiating the rungs obscured by his ample beer belly. But, with the magnified vision of his reading glasses, his equilibrium was askew.

"Watch out. Be careful," Evelyn called out with each measured step he took.

"Don't worry about me. I'm a professional." When he finally

reached the top, Lester found his breathing labored, no surprise after a winter of inactivity. This made him feel even dizzier. Mustn't lose this sale, he repeated to himself.

"Now, you see right here..." As Lester turned to point out the area above the flashing near the roof line, his knees wobbled and his body wavered. The ladder slowly pulled away from the house. With arms flailing, he threw himself toward the chimney and managed to grasp the cap piece above with both hands as the ladder left his feet below.

"Oh, my Lord! What do I do?" Evelyn cried.

"Get the ladder! Get the ladder!" he barked. But in just seconds, Lester would be back on the ground without the assistance of the ladder. Lester would be on the ground beneath a stack of bricks, a stack that only moments before had functioned as a chimney.

Evelyn stood frozen with a hand held over her gaping mouth. When the reality of what she had witnessed registered, she scurried up the porch steps and bolted straight for the kitchen. Lifting the phone receiver, she pressed the top button from a panel of ten speed-dial selections.

"Perkins and Sutherland Law Office," a cheerful voice answered.

"This is an emergency. I'd like to speak to Wendell Vance, your junior partner. This is his mother calling." While on hold, Evelyn gazed out the window to see if she could detect any movement from the pile of bricks.

"Mom, what's wrong?" Evelyn heard Wendell say.

"Son, I have to ask you. If my chimney fell down and somebody got hurt, who should be sued?"

"Mom, why do you ask? I thought you had the chimney repaired last year?"

"I did. Now tell me, who's liable?"

"It's somewhat complicated, but bottom line...the guy who made the repairs is the one you want to go after. Do you remember who did it?"

"Just a moment, Wendell." Evelyn crossed the kitchen tile to the refrigerator, portable phone in hand. There, amid a gallery of magnet-mounted photos of her grandchildren and their hand-drawn artwork, she found what she was looking for.

"Why yes, I do. I can't believe I saved this worthless old business card."

"What's the name on the card?"

"Lester Crone, Mr. Fix-It," she said with a trace of a smile.

KEVIN GILLOGLY has been a full-time advertising and promotional writer for more than twenty years. His published works include magazine articles, film and television criticism, humor pieces and editorials. He has contributed entries to the *Encyclopedia of Film* and *The Motion Picture Annual*. A game show junkie, he has competed on five different TV quiz shows.

Traveling On

Glynn Marsh Alam

Everything was gravestone gray—ground, buildings, sky and rectangular slabs, some cracked, some with faded epitaphs, but all gray, matching. Francine studied these pieces of granite, where an occasional blade peeked between the tiny spaces created by end-to-end stone. She imagined stringy corpses in rotted eighteenth-century gowns lying beneath the ground, clutching crosses and crumbling Bibles in bony hands. She bent over one end of a cracked slab, trying to make out the tribute to a family whose name began with *H*—or maybe it was *M*. The stone surface had eroded almost to the level of etching.

"Francy," Lydia Miller whispered in her old lady's voice, "you ought not to stand on a grave. You know what Grannie used to say!"

Francine jerked away from her thin-haired sister. "Stop nagging, Lydia. It's different in England. You saw all those tombs inside cathedrals. They walk over the dead here."

"Francy!"

"What?"

"You're standing on some writing. Get off!"

Francine looked down at her feet, clad in heavy walking shoes, not the style of Queen Elizabeth's Balmoral clunkers, but the therapeutic kind made for old ladies with arthritis. Her anger rose—directed at old age or her sister, she wasn't sure which—and she moved on to decipher more faded letters above an eighteenth-century date. Her sister tugged at her sleeve.

"Lydie, you're getting on my nerves!" Francine hissed. "Look around you. Nobody cares where we walk. These people have been dead too long. Even Grannie is fresher than they are."

Francine knew that last part would anger her sister. But at least, she'd clam up for a while.

"You evil old bag!" Lydia said.

"We're on vacation. Do you know what that word means? Or do you feel too guilty about spending Grannie's money? It's our money now. And we deserve this trip."

"I'm going back to the pub and have some tea," Lydia said. "You can walk over as many ghosts as you wish."

Lydia turned and picked up the walking cane she always carried, but seldom used. She wound amongst granite slabs and tilting headstones, then moved down the hill toward the pub.

Beyond her on the cobblestones of the main road, Francine could see two large tour buses, one for the Mississippi Retired Persons and the other for the Alabama Retirees. Her sister skirted the back of the buses and headed for the Black Bull Pub. When she saw the last of Lydia's double-knit suit, Francine turned back to the stones. "Good riddance!"

"Ma'am?"

Francine jumped. A man near her age, dressed in the British gentry style of a cricket aficionado—ascot, sport jacket, white shoes, straw hat—turned toward her. For a second, Francine thought she was seeing the Reverend Turner from back home.

"Oh, I'm so sorry. I was talking to myself, I guess." She felt her face flush. The heat rushed down her neck and she imagined ugly red splotches standing out on her chest. Secretly thankful for the blue wool turtleneck she was wearing, she followed her apology with a smile.

"I thought you were talking about the poor soul under that

slab," the man began, a half smile giving away his humor. "Why would he be a *good riddance* to you? I wonder."

"No, I meant..." Francine started to gesture in the direction of her sister, but thought better of it. Instead, she changed the subject. "How do you know it's a *he* buried under this slab?"

The man was smiling again. "I don't, really." He moved toward the stone as Francine stepped off the faded etching.

"Are you a teacher?" she asked, not knowing what else to say.

"No, but you are."

"How did you know?" Francine wrapped her arms around herself.

"Two ladies traveling from America—the South, I believe—to see the place where the Brontë sisters lived and wrote. Am I correct?"

"Yes."

"Fenton Harriman, at your service." The man, a stranger even if he did remind her of the sweet Reverend Turner, doffed his hat and firmly grasped her hesitant hand.

"Francine Miller, from Kelton, Mississippi. So you have met my sister?"

"She's your sister, then? I noticed the two of you walking together. I surmised you were traveling together. Miller—an English name, I believe."

"Yes, our ancestors mostly came from Britain." Francine felt her cheeks burn. Fenton was still holding her hand; she gently removed it and again wrapped her arms around herself.

"From this part?"

"South Yorkshire. Many people from there migrated to America years ago."

"Ah, yes. Discontented bunch. Are you more content now?"

"Content?" Francine shrugged. "It was many generations back, sir. I never migrated anywhere. Content? I couldn't really say."

But Francine had never been content. One of two sisters left in the care of an aging grandmother, she grew up in Baptist territory, where they were not allowed the social life so characteristic of Southern belles. No dancing, no makeup, no dating. Grannie was strict about all three. *If you go to dances now, you'll want to go when you're grown.* Francine always wondered why dancing was so bad for adults. Church had been their social life, until Grannie had interfered when the kind Reverend Turner showed Francine some affection. *It isn't proper to spend so much time alone with a man!*

"Have you been to England before?"

"Never." *Nor anywhere else, sir! And we wouldn't be here now if it weren't for Grannie's old trust fund she left to Uncle Willie. Only when he died, did we get the piddling leftovers.*

"Then surely you'll walk the hills to Top Withens?"

"I will?"

"Yes, you must. That's where the ruins of the old house are, the one Emily Brontë used as a model for *Wuthering Heights.*"

"Oh, yes, I would like to see that. I taught that book for years. So did my sister."

"Would your sister want to join us?"

Francine thought about that time forty years ago when Lydia sided with Grannie over Reverend Turner. How she wished she could have come on this trip without her.

"I don't think so. She carries—uses—a cane and doesn't like walking."

"Good! Then you will come with me?"

Harriman smiled shyly in invitation. His manner, boyish yet seductive, reminded her of a brief, happy time. Reverend Turner, a widower in much demand, had taken her thirty-year-old hand in both of his and asked her to walk with him. They strolled through the moss-draped gravestones behind the Baptist church, finally stopping by the old well. Green with algae and filled with stagnant water, it still provided a place for lovers to toss in a penny wish. The reverend had brushed her cheek with his hand, then leaned toward her. But she never received his kiss. Grannie's gasp put a halt to it. Later, the old woman would speak in anger. *You've gone too far, Francy.*

"Yes, I'd love to," she told Harriman, blushing at her own quick acceptance. "How far is the walk?"

"Follow me."

Fenton Harriman guided Francine away from the Brontë Parsonage and the bordering village of Haworth toward a dirt path that meandered among deep heather. They walked on the isolated road for a long time. The sky was still overcast, but no wind blustered about them, as Emily Brontë had described in her classic. Francine imagined she was Catherine—Fenton Harriman, Heathcliff—and she dreamed of a youthful romp through the heather. At times, Fenton took on the aura of the reverend, and her arm in his comforted her. It was only when Harriman walked in front of her that she remembered Reverend Turner's goodbye and his slumped back walking away from her. He had accepted Grannie's demand that he leave her granddaughter alone and left their little church with its stagnant wishing well. She heard he took up the calling in Texas somewhere, but she never saw him again.

When the road brought them to the bottom of a steep hill, Francine hesitated.

"Are we going up that path?"

"Have to. Top Withens is over this hill and on top of the next. It's probably the path Catherine took, certainly one that Emily Brontë knew." He smiled again. "Stay with me, we'll get there."

Fenton pushed on at a steady pace. Francine soon ran out of breath and stopped frequently to rest her burning legs and catch some of the cool, damp air in her lungs. She was beginning to wonder why she had come. Maybe because the alternative was to spend the day arguing with Lydie.

When they reached the top of the hill, Francine looked far out over fields of green heather that would soon turn purple. The wind had begun to blow slightly; it was almost icy compared to Mississippi, and just as damp. Taking in long gulps, she calmed her trembling leg muscles. In the distance, Francine caught a glimpse of white-washed stone farmhouses, their rocky yards surrounded by post fences, a few sheep grazing nearby. On a neighboring hill, a group of hikers trudged up one of the paths similar to the one she was on now.

"It's absolutely glorious! I'm going to suffer for this tomorrow, but right now, I'm so pleased you brought me here," she said. She briefly felt as though Reverend Turner had again taken her to a secluded spot.

"It is lovely, isn't it? But we need to move along. Have to go down, then up again."

"Why aren't the other people on our path?"

"There are different roads, but we took the one nearest the Brontë Parsonage. To reach the others requires a motor car."

"I see."

"We have to push on, then retrace our steps. If we stop, it will be nightfall before we make it back."

"It's just so steep!"

"Yes, but you'll be pleased when you've reached your destination."

As they climbed the final hill, intermittent red flashes blurred Francine's vision. Her heart pounded and her thigh muscles burned as though they would disintegrate. "I must sit down!"

"Top Withens is just beyond the heather. Stay with me."

"I just can't, Mr. Harriman. My legs won't move."

"Certainly they will. Here, let me help you."

"No, please..." But she allowed Harriman to drag her through the heather.

When finally they came to a cluster of stones shaped into a crude square, probably once a fireplace, Fenton stopped abruptly and let go of Francine's arm.

"Here we are."

Francine could barely breathe, her mouth hung open, and a foggy wheeze rose from her throat each time she pulled in oxygen. Again, red streaks flashed before her eyes and her head ached. Her heart worried her more than anything else. It pounded as though the entire valley could hear it. Collapsing on the ground in a mound of heather, she stared straight up at the sky, thankful for the cold mist that had begun to cling to her skin. She closed her eyes and listened to her heart for a long time. When finally it seemed she could sit up, she did so slowly, her head swimming with the rush of blood. "Whatever possessed me to do this?" For a moment, she saw a flash of Grannie hoeing weeds, shaking her head and frowning. *You've gone too far, Francy.* Blinking, she banished the image and focused on her immediate surroundings. She looked for Fenton, but he was nowhere in sight.

The heather was all around her so that when she tried to push herself up, she slipped twice, the second time coming down hard on her wrist.

"Mr. Harriman, I am going to need help!"

There was no reply. Forcing her aging body to a sitting position, Francine parted the heather, finding the old fireplace stones directly in front of her.

"So this is Wuthering Heights?"

Mr. Harriman was not in her line of sight. "Maybe he's walking around the ruins somewhere."

Slowly, Francine heaved herself to her feet. "Mr. Harriman," she called. Francine's white pants were smeared with damp earth, her jacket crumpled from lying in the moor grass. When she put her left hand to her head, her arm ached. She saw spots again. *It was foolish to walk up here just to see some old ruins. I'm nothing but an old ruin myself,* she thought.

"Mr. Harriman!" She called his name several times, her shaky voice echoing over the hill. Sharp pain stabbed her temple each time she shouted. Fenton Harriman had disappeared.

Mustn't wander too far. There are bogs on the moors. Francine remembered reading about animals that had become trapped in a kind of quickbog up here and had never been seen since. She flashed back to an old Sherlock Holmes movie where Watson had been stuck in a bog, then rescued, of course, by Holmes. *So where is my Holmes?* she wondered. Her heart began to pound again and she had to sit down once more in the heather.

She dozed off. When she awoke, the sky was growing dark. *Rain or night approaching?* After one more shout to Mr. Harriman, she gave up waiting and struck out on her own. Locating the path, she headed down, her knees buckling under her weight. The path was dark now, glorious heather transformed into menacing shadows. Francine could see no lights.

***

"Where is she?" Lydia screamed at Thomas Pettigrew, the Mississippi Retired Persons tour guide who had scheduled their trip, reserved their hotel rooms, and nursed them through aches, grumbles and cathedrals all the way from London. Three tour groups had crowded into the lobby of the inn, elderly tourists waiting for the evening meal. A pall seemed to envelop the room when they heard Francine was missing.

"I think I saw her talking to a man in the graveyard," said Grace, a tiny woman from the Alabama Retirees tour group, who never looked up from her knitting. "Maybe they went to dinner."

"My sister doesn't dine with strange men!"

"Just in case, I checked all the pubs around here. She's not there. Miss Miller, was—is—your sister well? I mean, is there any chance she could have fainted somewhere?" Thomas began to sweat as he faced the missing woman's sister.

"Miller women do not faint. Someone got her, I'm sure. I've heard of terrorists taking American hostages. They probably think she's some wealthy old hen. Well, just let me get to a phone and call the embassy. We'll see what happens next!" Lydia's chin trembled in spite of her threat.

"No need for that, Miss Miller. Haworth is not a popular locale for terrorists. I've asked the clerk at the inn to check the clinic. Maybe she is ill."

"Or wandered onto the moors. She was going down a path away from the cemetery the last time I saw her—with that man." Grace from Alabama continued to knit, not pausing as she lifted her face to smile briefly, her eyes darting up and back.

"You saw her and never said anything?" Lydia's eyes narrowed.

"I didn't know until now that you were looking for her," said Grace, her needles clicking louder.

"Can you stop knitting long enough to talk seriously about this? She is my sister, after all!" Lydia raised her cane halfway off the floor, as if she were going to hit someone.

"I can knit and talk. My dear late husband always said I could. Said I always saw things I wasn't supposed to see, too." She stopped knitting and gazed over the heads of her fellow travelers.

"I think I should call the constable." Thomas fled the room, dabbing at his sweating face in spite of the damp cold.

Outside in the cemetery, the slabs, pitch black, formed a dark union with the large trees that surrounded them. It was impossible to see anyone stumbling on top of the ancient graves in front of the Brontë manse, just a few steps behind the village shops. Heavy mist and night clouds obliterated any sign of the moon. Even the Parsonage museum, which burned a light outside the front door, was shrouded in darkness, the bulb a yellow haze in the heavy fog. It would have been deadly quiet if not for an occasional owl that dared to sound a call. At the bottom of the hill and down the cobbled street, the inn was ablaze, its inhabitants alive with alarm, for one of theirs was missing.

***

Francine lay face up, her heart drumming into the stone beneath her back. She sensed everything. Small pieces of cracked granite stuck into her skin through her heavy jacket. She smelled the odor of rotting earth where unclean water had sickened the Brontë sisters years ago. Small beetles crawled across her torn pants. Leaves rustled in the tree above her.

"My purse...I forgot my purse," she whispered. She heard Grannie's voice order her to go back and find it, but the reverend smiled and told her he'd bring it along. She remembered long-ago details of her Southern home. Swamp water, dark and stagnant, muggy heat as damp as an algae-covered well, and moss hanging over white stones, her dear reverend's voice close by in the night singing "Rock of Ages." Such a sweet sound, she moved her mouth along with his.

"...cleft for me...let me hide...myself in..." Her mouth closed abruptly, her eyes still open, unblinking.

***

"What happened?" whispered one plump lady tourist with dyed red hair to a portly, bow-legged man who stood beside her at the edge of the cemetery. Brontë manse guards were helping the constable rope off the burial ground with yellow tape.

"A woman collapsed in the graveyard," the portly man said. "It looks like she's dead."

"How did she die? Do they know?" Another tourist spoke in a whisper.

"I told you, she went off with a man. They should be looking for him, too. He could have collapsed somewhere." Grace from Alabama spoke grimly, her knitting tucked into her white Brontë Parsonage tote as she stood with her group. "People have to watch out for themselves, especially when they get to be our age."

Lydia walked away from the center of the cemetery, rage on her face along with tears. "I told her again and again. I told her to mind our Grannie. But she just wouldn't listen." Her bitter voice drifted away from the others as she made her way down the hill to a waiting police car.

***

The Alabama Retirees tour bus pulled out of Haworth, its tires bumping over the ancient cobblestones, gears grinding as it eased almost straight downhill away from the inn, the pub and the Brontë Parsonage. The tour guide stood next to the driver's seat, microphone in hand, explaining Heptonstall, "location of the oldest Methodist church still in use and the burial place of your American poet, Sylvia Plath. It also features the ruins of a large abbey with hundreds of granite slabs. One could spend an entire day just reading the inscriptions on those old stones," he said.

And old stones were the attraction in the high village built on a steep slope, an abbey right out of a horror movie. White-haired gentlemen clung to bent women with frizzy perms. Blue-haired ladies in double-knit suits and running shoes stumbled off the bus and onto the slabs to see who had passed on before the time of King George III. They didn't look up to see tiny Grace from Alabama chatting with an elderly gentleman wearing an ascot and white shoes.

Fenton Harriman tipped his straw hat to Grace, who noticed how his eyes twinkled when he smiled—just like her late husband's. He asked, "Would you care to walk down the hill with me to see the oldest Methodist church still in use?"

GLYNN MARSH ALAM is the English department chair at Los Angeles High School, where she teaches writing and English literature. She has contributed stories to *Back Porch* and *Thema* magazines and has won awards for her writing at the Southwest Writers' Conference, California Writers' Conference and Philadelphia Writers' Conference.

Never Heard the Shot That Killed Him

Larry Hill

"One shot," Meyer said. "Small caliber, probably some vari-ant of a twenty-two. Came through the window there." Hunt followed Doc Meyer's motion to the small hole in the middle of the floor-to-ceiling window. "Lived long enough to try to tell us who tapped him."

Hunt stared at the bloody pictograph near Tom O'Donnell's hand. "Looks like a heart with a slash through it. No heart? Heart-less?"

"Or a valentine?"

"Knowing O'Donnell, he was wishing me another Happy Valentine's Day."

"That's the day she left, eh?"

"You mean the day he made her go."

Meyer tore the wrapper from a sterile scalpel, made a small incision below O'Donnell's ribcage and inserted a round-faced ther-mometer into the liver. "Didn't want her to marry a cop. Probably had his reasons."

"Yeah, he didn't think I was good enough for her."

Meyer sat back on his heels and noted the liver temperature on his clipboard. "Heard she married a professor."

"That so?" Hunt walked to the window. He imagined a line of

sight from the body through the jagged hole in the window across the small inlet separating Tom O'Donnell's chalet from the narrow road hugging Lac du Coeur. A red Miata rounded a bend in the narrow road and stopped. Hunt turned from the window. "Someone waited on Shoreline Road. Waited until the fat boy gave him a perfect shot. Then, bang. Lights out."

Meyer stood and rubbed his knees. "I almost forgot, Smitty said they're in town. At The Bear Inn. If you're interested."

Hunt stepped out to the deck. Staring into algae-green water, he remembered his last night with Maggie. The sunset burned orange over the reaches of the pines, all reflected on the icy surface of Lac du Coeur. She was angry because he wouldn't stand up to her father, because he wouldn't take her away. There were no words to explain, and he knew he'd never see her again.

Meyer joined him on the deck. "Can I get him out of here?"

"You better, the buzzards are circling." Hunt lit a cigarette and pointed to two women exiting the red Miata stopped at the side of the road.

Meyer smiled. "Big news when a retired cop gets it in his own living room." He nodded to the gurney-jockeys waiting by the M.E.'s van and returned to the chalet.

"Hey, Dennis," Sue Kern shouted. He nodded, hoping his plastic smile masked his distaste for *The Sentinel* reporter. "Someone croak O'Donnell?"

Hunt glared. Before he could answer, she continued. "I'm not going to dance with you on this one, Dennis. Give me something or I go straight to the old man, and you know how that's going to end."

"Another crack like that and you don't even get the weekly crime report. See how the old man likes that."

"You're making one hell of an impression." Sue glanced at the petite redhead at her side. "Laura Kirkpatrick, reporter, meet Dennis Hunt, detective with a big chip on his shoulder."

He shrugged and flipped his cigarette butt into the lake. "When

I'm ready to make a statement, you'll be the first to know. Until then, no effing comment." He marched down the steps and passed the reporters.

She answered the door after one knock and offered a weak smile. Ten years had passed since she'd boarded a bus to anywhere he and her father weren't. She hadn't changed. Maybe her hips were a little wider, but he couldn't be sure. Her thick, blond hair still hung loosely over her shoulders in that casually elegant way it did in his memory, but her deep blue eyes were red-rimmed and puffy. He felt as if someone had gut-punched him.

"It's good of you to come, Dennis," she said, an edge betraying her true feelings.

Over her shoulder, Hunt saw Smitty standing with a lanky man who peered above half-rim glasses at the open door.

"Could you step into the hall, please?"

She sighed with displeasure but followed Hunt to the hotel corridor.

"I'm here to inform you that your father—"

"I already know."

"Smitty had no authority—" He wanted to grab his words in mid-air and pull them back, but it was too late.

"I wondered how you'd be. Now I know." Her face flushed with anger.

"This is official police business."

"Don't give me that crap. Of all days...Daddy's been murdered." She started to turn back into the room. "And Smitty didn't tell us."

Hunt searched the empty hallway looking for some way to reach Maggie. "This isn't pleasant for either of us," he said softly. "But I have a job to do."

"How gallant. The man on the white steed. Get off it, Dennis." She tramped into the suite.

Hunt followed and, with a withering glance, sent Smitty scurrying out of the room.

"Honey, this is Dennis Hunt. Dennis, my husband, Dr. Noel Valentine."

"I wish I could say I was happy to meet you," Valentine said, extending his hand.

Hunt shook it. "I have to ask a few questions."

"I was just telling Officer Smith—"

"I'm not interested in what you were telling him."

"Understood."

"When did you and your wife arrive in Lac du Coeur?"

"Yesterday afternoon. About four. The hotel should have a record."

"Did you stop at the chalet?"

"No. We met for dinner at the Lakeview, then called it an early night."

"Did your father-in-law appear troubled?"

"I wouldn't say so."

"Why now?"

"He asked us to come," Maggie answered.

"And?"

"You know how he was. The less said, the better."

"What'd you think?"

The couple exchanged glances. "We thought he was dying," Maggie said.

"Not him." For the second time in minutes, Hunt wished he had the power to rewind time. He tried to explain. "Thought he'd outlive me just to spit on my grave."

"You'll never get it, will you?" Maggie asked. "He didn't like you because you were just like him. That's why I left. I didn't need two fathers."

They drifted into an awkward silence. "I may need to see you both again," Hunt said, and left.

Returning to the small brick building the Lac du Coeur Police Department called headquarters, he phoned the Los Angeles Police Department's records division. They promised O'Donnell's arrest summary and personnel file by noon.

He called Smitty into his office. "Anybody new in town?"

"A few. Kern and her friend, the redhead. Bill Thomas, up on Vista View. Hunters. A few real estate speculators."

"Check them out. Get back to me as soon as possible before Hacker loses it."

Smitty laughed and left to make his calls.

Finished with the preliminary entries in the O'Donnell murder book, Hunt leaned back in his wooden chair. His mind raced after meaning. No heart. Heartless. A valentine. At whom was O'Donnell pointing? Noel Valentine? Or was it something else?

Through his window, he watched some kids playing pile-on in Connie Wright's front yard. They had no dead bodies and no lost loves. They had nothing but the time to have fun.

Chief Hacker's entrance interrupted Hunt's speculations. "We need to talk." He led the way to his office and motioned Hunt into a chrome chair while he wedged himself behind his clean desk.

Hunt surveyed Hacker's office and for the thousandth time wondered why Hacker surrounded himself with trophies.

"The mayor phoned. Says we already made the wire service and the Los Angeles news. He's damn unhappy about it. Says the next thing you know, real estate prices'll start falling. Nobody wants that. If he wasn't my brother—" Hacker stopped in mid-sentence. "Well, never mind that. He wants us to find the killer, pronto. I'm going to ride you hard on this one. How's it look?"

"Could be a pro. Whoever pulled the trigger wanted him dead and knew how to accomplish the task with a minimum of fuss."

"What about this message he left?"

"We're trying to keep that quiet."

"Don't pick nits, Detective." Hacker leaned forward on his beefy arms.

"He was trying to tell us who killed him."

"And?"

"And I hope the answer comes in from L.A. this afternoon."

"And if not?"

"We look for someone with a grudge against a retired cop."

"What?" Hacker's face turned crimson and with it his voice became a squeal. "We've got over a hundred-fifty retired police officers living out their years here, sixty from L.A. alone. Don't tell me you think we've got a wacko on the loose."

"I didn't say that."

Hacker leaned back and closed one eye as he considered what Hunt told him. After a few minutes, he nodded. "Reports twice daily. See you back here at five."

Hunt returned to his desk. Marylou Corazon, the only civilian employee of the Lac du Coeur Police Department, stuck her head in to say that his L.A. fax was printing. Hunt nodded and slipped on his jacket. "I'm going over to Slim's for a coffee. Want anything?" Marylou shook her head.

"Hey there." Sue Kern's metallic voice hurt his ears.

"Not you again? You've been around less than six months and it feels like a lifetime."

She walked across the empty diner and stood next to him. Her heavy perfume made his head ache. "Ready to make a statement?"

Though Hunt didn't like her much, he appreciated her directness. "No."

"You can do better than that." Her amber eyes narrowed with the challenge.

"There's nothing to release."

"So, you sit here drinking coffee, doing nothing. Is that the kind of story you want to read? Is that the kind of story the mayor wants to read?"

"Why don't you write: 'Reporter Solves Murder'?"

"Point made. But tell me something."

He answered carefully. "We don't know what kind of bullet killed O'Donnell yet. I can't think of anyone in Lac du Coeur who'd want to kill him. Or a reason. You got any ideas?"

"Had to be someone new in town."

"Why? Why not someone who lived here all their life?"

"All right. You win."

"Even if *you* did it, I'd have to figure out why and then place you there at the right time with the means. So, until I find out some history on O'Donnell, I can't do or say anything. Now, if you don't mind, I'd like to finish my coffee and maybe even have a cigarette."

Sue started for the door. "I'll go pump Doc Meyer. He's an old faucet, anyway."

"Don't worry, Bob. I know. I know. I'll call you. Goodbye." Hacker put down the phone and looked at Hunt. "The damn phone hasn't stopped ringing all day. That was Bob Foran informing me of the real estate implications. Murder in Lac du Coeur is bad enough, but a retired cop who moves here for safety and comfort, cut down in his living room. There's almost a panic out there."

"One murder every two years isn't a panic situation, Chief."

"I know that, Hunt. But the good folks of Lac du Coeur don't. They aren't willing to accept any murders."

Hunt nodded.

"What'd you get from L.A.?"

"You want the short version?"

"The whole thing."

"O'Donnell earned seven commendations—not bad for a twenty-five-year career. He was forced to retire as a result of a disciplinary action, a bad shoot."

"What happened?"

"There's not much in the file. O'Donnell shot a twelve-year-old kid, and the records were sealed by court order."

"Get those records."

"I hadn't thought of that, sir." Hunt said, not completely hiding his derision.

"What else?" Hacker glowered.

"I looked for hearts, valentines, anything. Got three hits that turned out to be misses."

"Don't stop there."

"Angela Hartfield, while drunk, stabbed her husband with garden shears when he accidentally stepped on her prize-winning Shih Tzu. Died during a prison riot ten years ago."

"Lovely woman."

Hunt continued: "Leslie Valentino killed her husband after he beat her. Shot him in the head. She's in the California Women's Colony, Norco."

"Some men deserve killing."

"Wouldn't say that to the newspapers, sir."

"Never mind that, get on with it."

"Hart Lankersham poisoned his wife for her insurance money. During his arrest at a Hollywood bar, there was a scuffle and he killed a cop. Fell between the cracks when California abolished the death penalty. He's in a level-four block at San Quentin."

"Not much, is it?"

"Just dead ends."

"Well, find something. I'm up to my ass in alligators."

"Smitty made a few calls. Maggie's husband's apparently made some bad investments. They're almost broke. Then there's that damn reporter."

Hacker interrupted: "Valentine discovered the body."

"What?" Hunt felt his face flush with anger. "Son of a bitch!"

"My fault, Dennis. I got the call. Forgot to tell you with all the excitement." Hacker paused. "You think Tom was trying to tell us his son-in-law whacked him?"

Hunt wanted to blast the chief, but his anger quickly dissipated as he imagined the pain in Maggie's eyes when she discovered her husband was a killer. He stated his reasoning aloud. "You know the old saw: Odds are even that the person who finds the body is the killer. Combine that with the valentine and a small inheritance going to Maggie."

"Strikes two and three."

"I'll get Smitty to check Kansas City and area for gun purchases."

"Won't help if he picked it up on the street," Hacker commented. Hunt nodded. "What were you saying about a reporter?"

"Nothing important."

Hunt left Hacker's office and stepped out of the station for a smoke. He walked across the parking lot wondering why more things weren't as easy as solving a murder.

"Wait up." Hunt watched the redhead cross the street.

"I'm Laura Kirkpatrick."

"I remember."

She extended her hand and he took it. It was soft and warm. "You're with the *Times*."

"That's right. I was hoping you might give me a statement. Do you have any suspects? Was O'Donnell working anything for you?"

Hunt held his hand up to stop her. "The *Times* said they never heard of you."

"What'd you expect?" She smiled. "L.A. is not as friendly as Lac du Coeur. People are raped and murdered every day after someone gets an address, a phone number, from some well-meaning fool. *Times* policy says if your name doesn't appear on the list, you get nothing, not even an acknowledgment of employment."

Hunt shrugged. "You'll need to contact the paper so I can verify your identity."

"No prob."

"What brings you to Lac du Coeur?"

"I'm working on a story about retired L.A. cops. It's my ticket to bigger and better."

"Why here?"

"For the time being, I'd rather not say."

"I'll be the judge of that. It may have something to do with a murder."

"Then an answer with a question. What in this little hamlet attracts so many retired cops? Must be something."

Hunt had never thought about it. "A million miles from old memories?"

"So is Bakersfield and it's mucho closer to civilization." She looked past Hunt to the mountains surrounding the lake. "There's something else here. Something only old cops know."

"Like what?"

"Forgiveness?"

Hunt rolled his eyes.

"So it's the fresh air." She laughed. "Got any dinner plans?"

Hunt rolled out of bed and stumbled to the bathroom. His head ached and his mouth reminded him of old felt, dry and dusty. He turned on the water, stepped under the shower, leaned against the wall and let hot water run over his head. A long red hair circled the drain at his feet. Suddenly, he was very much awake. He jumped from the shower, wrapped himself in a towel and ran down to the kitchen.

"Breakfast's almost ready. Kiss me and get dressed."

He kissed her and went upstairs to dress. When he returned to the kitchen, not quite sure what to say, she was gone. She left a note on his plate. "Lovely dinner. Exquisite dessert. Call me when you can. I'm at The Bear Inn. Laura." Maggie O'Donnell was a million miles away.

Hunt hit the answering machine play button and recognized Meyer's voice. "Found the bullet, a twenty-two Hornet, lodged in the spine. They're not too common, but they aren't exotic, either. Pierced O'Donnell's lower aorta. I'll send the official report when I finish it. By the way, I talked to Sue Kern last night. She's a lovely girl. You ought to ask her out for dinner sometime."

Hunt was still muttering to himself when the phone rang. He was in no mood for games or chitchat. "Yeah?"

"Rough night?"

"What is it, Smitty?"

"You'd better get over here. Bob Johnson's dead."

Hunt sped up the long twisty road to Bob Johnson's ranch house. Smitty met him in Johnson's driveway.

"What happened?"

"See for yourself."

They walked to the back of the house. Smitty pointed to Bob Johnson's corpse in the grass next to his lawn mower.

"Came out to cut his grass. Somebody sat up the hill there." Smitty pointed to the wooded rise a hundred feet away. "One shot through the heart."

"Did you call Meyer?"

"Called you first."

"Call Meyer." Smitty started to walk to his car. "Wait awhile. How'd you happen up here?"

"Just stopped to visit. Thought I'd see about this week's poker game."

Hunt knew sugar coating when he heard it. "Bullshit."

Smitty shifted his feet, pushed his cap back and rubbed his forehead. "Johnson and O'Donnell were partners."

"And?"

"Bill Thomas was their old supervisor. He moved up here last month."

Hunt swallowed his anger. "Next time, check with me first. Call Meyer."

Hunt walked away from Johnson's body up the hill. Fifteen feet in from the tree line there were ill-defined footprints. Whoever left them wasn't a big person. He placed a marker by the prints and followed them up to the road above. He marked a tire track in the graveled shoulder and walked down the road back to Johnson's house.

Word spread fast. Angry ex-cops called, some fearing their nightmares had come true, some afraid that Hunt wasn't up to the task of discovering the killer; the rest threatening to form a vigilante group if Hunt didn't get some results pretty damn quick. Marylou gave him a reason to ignore the phone when she brought Johnson's records.

Johnson had retired after a rocky career: nine reprimands and two suspensions for excessive force. He'd been O'Donnell's partner, but there couldn't have been two more different cops.

Hunt wondered if Thomas might provide the link to their deaths. He phoned but got no answer. He felt that black hole in his stomach, put down the phone and ran to his Blazer. Racing up the mountain, he wished the Chevy could move as fast as his thoughts.

He stepped from the cab. Something was wrong. He sensed it. He drew his Smith & Wesson, moved cautiously toward the front door and rang the doorbell. He heard a noise on the other side. No mistaking it, someone had cocked an automatic. He stepped to the side and knocked again.

"Who is it?" a gruff voice demanded.

"Dennis Hunt."

"Door's open. Make it slow, as if your life depended on it, 'cause it does."

Hunt pushed the door open with his foot. Bob Thomas, a thin man, with thinning hair and an aquiline nose, stood at the back of the hall with a 9mm automatic in his hand.

Hunt showed his badge and barked, "Put the frigging gun down."

"You're in my house uninvited. I shoot you, no questions asked. Shut the door."

Hunt kicked the door closed without taking his eyes off Thomas and wondered if he'd blundered into a trap.

"Put your piece on the table there," Thomas said, motioning to a cherry stand by the door, "and keep your hands where I can see them."

Hunt glanced around, looking for a place to move.

"Put the damn gun down."

Hunt stepped to the table and placed his gun on it. "You're making a mistake."

"That's ripe. Listen, cracker, I ain't dying for being stupid. That's one thing you learn on the streets I come from." Thomas's anger fixed a wall between them.

It was the kind of anger Hunt knew well. No amount of reasoning would dissipate it, but he had to try. "What's frightening you?"

"I'll ask the questions. What're you doing here?"

"I didn't get any answer."

"And you thought I might be dead?"

Hunt stared.

"Well, I'm not."

Hunt nodded. "I called to find out what you know about a bad shoot. A young boy was killed—"

"You think O'Donnell and Johnson got whacked for that? No way. Too long ago."

"What's your theory?"

"I don't have one." Thomas lowered his gun.

"I don't buy that. Not the way you're acting."

Thomas pursed his lips, thinking. "It's got to be revenge."

Hunt nodded. "O'Donnell wrote something that looked like a heart with a line through it. Mean anything to you?"

"This way." Thomas pointed his pistol toward a dimly lit room.

Hunt followed Thomas's motion into a windowless room. Thomas waved Hunt into a chair and then sat across from him.

"It was one of those nights. Everything was off. We all felt edgy. You know the feeling, like your ticket's been punched and you're just waiting for the train. We'd staked this restaurant. The bad guys were in or going in. When they came out, a kid ran with them. They fired. It was like a jungle fire fight." Thomas shook his head at an unseen vision. "Tom warned the kid and fired. Could've been any one of us." Thomas wiped his eye. "O'Donnell never tried to cover up. If ever a man felt remorse, it was him."

Hunt nodded. He had experienced O'Donnell's legendary moodiness, and he suddenly knew why O'Donnell had chased him from Maggie. He didn't want his daughter to deal with that kind of pain. "What happened to the boy's family?"

"The old man drank himself to death. Mother, son and daughter moved back to somewhere with a half-million dollars from the city."

"What were their names?"

"I thought I'd never forget them, but, like a lot of other things, they've slipped away." Thomas bent his head down. His slightness turned to frailty.

"The records are sealed," Hunt said. "And I need their names." Thomas moved his head as if he agreed. Hunt stood. "I better take this." He reached down and picked up Thomas's pistol. "Wouldn't want you to do anything stupid, like shoot the paperboy."

Wind rustled the pines outside his cabin. Someone knocked at the front door. Hunt started down the hall, stopped halfway and retraced his steps. Locked and loaded, he returned to the door and opened it a crack. Laura turned and smiled.

"Going to invite me in? Or kill me?"

"Sorry." He put the safety on and slipped the gun into his waistband before opening the door.

She breezed into his arms and kissed him slow and deep. "I've been thinking about you all day," she whispered in his ear. "Want to get some dinner? Or would you rather eat in?"

Hunt closed the door and led the way to his bedroom. "You're the first woman…"

"Sssh." She put her finger to his lips. "Show me."

Passion swept over them like a hot summer wind, lighting sparks in dark crevices that finally blazed up in a firestorm, leaving nothing but a smoldering emptiness.

Laura rested her head on Hunt's shoulder. After a long kiss, she asked him, "So? Who killed Tom O'Donnell and the other guy?"

"That why you came?"

"Which time?"

"You're disgusting." They both laughed. "I'm not sure. I'm

hoping their old supervisor will be able to help."

"What about the mark on the floor?"

"Don't know."

"So there was one?"

"You're sneaky."

"I'm a beautiful woman; if I wasn't sneaky, I'd never get anywhere."

"It was a heart with a line through it. Like this." Hunt traced the mark on her stomach.

"Like a brand."

"Hadn't thought of that. Heart Bar. Bar Heart. Doesn't help."

She climbed on top of him, her red hair falling over her breasts. "Want to play bucking bronco?"

It was after nine when Smitty called and told him to get out to Bill Thomas's house. He drove up to Vista View. Smitty's patrol car sat in the drive. Behind it was Meyer's Cadillac. Hunt knew Thomas was dead.

He walked to the front of the house. Thomas's body lay across the threshold, one bloodied hole in the back of his shirt.

"How long's he been dead?"

"He's in full rigor," Meyer replied from the hallway. "I'd say eight to twelve hours. I'll know better after I get him on the table. Look at these powder marks." Meyer pointed to a large spray pattern. "He was shot in the back at close range. Probably running away. Looks like a twenty-two again."

"Who found him?"

"Smitty. He's across the road."

Hunt walked across the road into the pine forest. He heard Smitty breaking twigs as he walked, and followed the sound. He found Smitty bent over a dull brass.

"Find something?"

"A shell casing. The killer stood over there." Smitty pointed to Hunt's right. Hunt found the small clearing, from which there was an unimpeded view of Thomas's front door. Smitty joined him.

"The killer may have stood here, but Meyer says Thomas was shot at close range."

"I guess this isn't important then." Smitty threw the brass into the woods.

"What brought you up here, Smitty?"

"Thomas asked me to bring him his gun."

"It was evidence," Hunt said.

"Not the way I saw it."

"Give me your badge."

"Hacker said I should follow my hunches."

"Give me your goddamn badge!"

Hunt returned to the office, exhausted. He'd stopped to ask the Valentines about their bankruptcy and spent the day lifting the lid off Maggie's marriage. Finally, he was satisfied that Noel Valentine hadn't killed his father-in-law and the others. Valentine had been stupid with his money, but he wasn't a killer. He also knew that Maggie would never speak to him again.

He collapsed in his chair and wished he had an office bottle. The message light blinked; he hit the play button. "Called in a few favors." It was Thomas's gruff voice. "A fax is headed your way."

"Thanks," Hunt said to the ghost of a dead cop.

Hunt walked to the fax machine, read the short message and ran to his Blazer. Part of him wished he was too late. Part of him wanted justice. He found what he was looking for in the Lakeview restaurant parking lot.

Maggie and Noel sat in a dark corner overlooking Lac du Coeur, whispering and holding hands. Smitty leaned on the bar, hoisting a shot glass high over his head. Across the small dining room, Laura and Sue laughed. They waved when they saw him.

Smitty grabbed his arm as he passed. "You're destroying my life."

"Go home, Smitty. Don't make a bad situation worse." Smitty stood his ground for a minute before staggering back to the bar.

Hunt walked to Laura's table. "Sit down, Dennis," Sue said. Hunt ignored her and drew his Smith & Wesson.

"I'm arresting you for the murders of Tom O'Donnell, Bob Johnson and Bill Thomas."

Sue laughed. "Who?"

"Laura Kirkpatrick, you have the right to—"

"You've got to be kidding," Sue said.

"I know what O'Donnell was trying to write. Hart K. He never finished."

"Come on, Dennis, the joke's over," Laura said.

"I can only imagine how it must hurt to lose a brother, the brother you protected."

"What are you talking about?" Sue asked.

"Hart Kirkpatrick, Laura's brother, was killed when he failed to stop at the scene of an armed robbery."

"He never heard them yelling," Laura cried. "He was deaf. He never even heard the shot that killed him."

"Come with me, Laura." She started to stand.

"You bastard," Smitty slurred. He spun Hunt around, took a swing and missed. Hunt pushed him down. When he turned around, Laura had vanished. Sue pointed to the deck. Hunt ran after her.

She leaned on the railing, staring into the dark water. "It was up to me." She paused. "My mother died two months ago. I hired a detective. He found Thomas. Imagine my surprise when I found them all here." She turned, the chrome pistol in her hand aimed at Hunt's chest. "They killed my brother. I killed them."

Hunt turned sideways to minimize his profile and aimed at her heart.

"Drop the gun," he yelled.

She pulled her trigger. Hunt fired. His bullet found its mark; hers went wide as she fell backward, through the railing, into Lac du Coeur.

Sue rushed out onto the deck.

Hunt stared in disbelief at the broken railing.

After a black silence, Sue said, "It was her way out, Dennis." She touched his arm.

"What about the rest of us?" Hunt walked into the restaurant and called Meyer.

LARRY HILL is a Seneca Indian from the Six Nations Reserve located in Ontario, Canada. He worked for a community newspaper as a sports editor and photographer before accepting a position as a government economist in Toronto. He moved to Los Angeles to again pursue his writing career. He now resides in Long Beach, where he writes for the local weekly newspaper.

Dying to Exhale

Sandy Siegel

He took a long drag on the cigarette. Then he exhaled, send-ing a puff of smoke out the car window. It was freezing outside—at least, by L.A. standards—but the open window was the only way she would allow him to smoke. A small price to pay for his free-dom.

She stared at the cancer stick pressed between his lips. Even with the window open, the car reeked of smoke. She coughed. Not that he would get the message. It would take more than a little hacking to get through to him. Much more.

"You oughta get that checked out," he said. "You could be coming down with something."

His sarcasm wasn't lost on her. She hacked some more—just to annoy him.

Ex-smokers. How he hated her theatrics—not to mention her holier-than-thou attitude. "If I could quit, so can you," she was always telling him. The fact is, he didn't want to quit. What was the point? If nicotine didn't get him, air pollution, pesticide poi-soning, contaminated meat, fatty foods and a host of other evil substances probably would. Shit, he could step off a sidewalk and a bus could do him in. Every day was a battle to stay alive; he chose to wage the war his way. If she didn't like it, she could leave. She *should* leave. She was the one screwing up the marriage. Everything was fine until she went on her crusade to make the world safe from tobacco.

He flicked the butt outside and hit the power-windows button.

"Not so fast," she said. "I'd like to be able to breathe."

"It's ice-cold in here."

"And the weather's pretty lousy, too."

"Touché," he said. At least, she hadn't totally lost her sense of humor.

Funny, to think it was actually cigarettes that had brought them together. In a coffee shop. He asked if he could bum one off her. One-and-a-half packs and three hours later they were making plans for the weekend. When he proposed six months later, he confessed his "I'm out of smokes" line was just an excuse to meet her. She confessed she knew. She went along for the ride—back then, she liked the idea of having her own personal Marlboro Man. Now, she wasn't proud of that fact. But what could she say? Smoke got in her eyes.

She turned to look at him. He didn't hold up when the haze cleared.

He glanced at the dashboard clock. They had been driving for twenty minutes; it would be another twenty before they arrived. She couldn't have picked a restaurant closer to home? Of course not, that would have been considerate. She did things like this simply to irritate him. Her excuse this time? Their tenth anniversary. That called for someplace special. Translation: small portions at high prices. If Spending Hubby's Hard-Earned Cash were an Olympic event, she'd be a gold medalist. He grabbed another cigarette from his pocket.

Always has enough money for coffin nails. But an anniversary present? Figures dinner is enough. And she'd expended so much time and cash coming up with the perfect surprise for him.

"Where the hell did you find this place?" he asked at their small corner table.

"Connie recommended it," she said.

"Connie. Now there's someone whose opinion I would really trust."

"Maybe if you loosened up and made some effort to enjoy things, instead of complaining all the time—"

"At these prices, I have a right to complain. I can't even get another lousy six-dollar glass of wine while I'm waiting for my twenty-two-dollar piece of dried-out fish. Did the waiter go home?"

"Give him a break. He has two large parties. Besides, yelling 'Hey, buddy!' is not the way to win his heart."

"I don't want his heart. I want a glass of wine," he said, pulling a cigarette from his jacket pocket.

"No smoking," she reminded him through gritted teeth.

"What gives the fucking government the right to tell me when and where I can smoke?"

As he nervously tapped the cigarette on the table, she trained her eyes on his.

"What?" he said.

"Nothing." She looked at her watch. "Why don't you go outside, honey?"

Her change of tone caught him off guard.

"Let's not fight anymore," she said. "Life is too short. Happy anniversary."

The way she smiled didn't sit right with him. But first things first.

***

He took one last drag, then tossed the butt on the sidewalk, crushing the smoldering remains with the bottom of his shoe.

He never saw the big blue car jump the curb.

"I don't believe it," she said between sobs.

"Drunk drivers," said a uniformed police officer, shaking his head in disgust.

"He'll probably get off with a slap on the wrist, while my husband—" She stopped as she choked back her tears.

"I'm sorry. Look, I'll get someone to take you home. Wait here."

As the policeman headed for a black-and-white, she dried her eyes and glanced at the culprit sitting in the back seat. He was a tall, thin guy with dirty-blond hair. She had pictured just the opposite—someone short, beefy and dark. Funny how people never look the way they sound. But what did it matter? He got the job done—the "accident" looked credible. His fee would more than compensate for the negligible punishment he would receive.

A female officer approached and said, "C'mon, ma'am, I'll take you home."

"Thanks. I appreciate it."

"Pretty rotten timing—coming out for a cigarette just then."

"Yes, it was."

She followed the officer to a second black-and-white, muttering to herself, "But I did warn him smoking was going to kill him."

SANDY SIEGEL has written for numerous TV sitcoms and dramas, as well as magazines and newspapers, including the *Los Angeles Times* and *Writer's Digest.* Her comic mystery novel, *Funny Business,* is currently making the rounds in New York.

Trickery

Judith Klerman Smith

"Murder shrieks," wrote playwright John Webster. He was right. I know, believe you me. Remember about two years ago, that murder of Rabbi Reuben Becker? Well, I was there. Oh, not actually in his study when he was murdered, but right outside when Hildy Newman, his secretary, started to shriek. See, that's what I mean. It's people who shriek. But murder can make lots of noise, too. I mean, when the police and concerned citizens like me find murderers and motives, that's when murder shrieks.

Who am I? I'm Bea Silver. Beatrice. Funny thing is, I am, you know, silver. I don't dye. I always say, a grandmother, even a young one (I'm only sixty) can look like a grandmother and still look good. I'm not very tall. (My husband, he should rest in peace, towered over me by half a foot, and he was only five feet ten inches.) I'm still slim like on the day I married, even after three kids.

"It's not from the wind you get fat," Momma used to say. So I eat like a bird and do tae kwon do religiously.

But, I digress. The five of us—Leigh Diamond, Harry Greenstone, Sylvia Freed, Hildy and I—were at B'nai Torah, one of the larger Orthodox synagogues (*shul*, we call it) in L.A., for our Bible class. (I like to exercise my mind so it doesn't atrophy.) We were waiting for the summons into the rabbi's study where we meet each Tuesday evening for our lesson, when Hildy volunteered to go see if he was ready for us.

The next thing we knew, Hildy's yelling, and Harry, Leigh and I are bumping into each other like Larry, Moe and Curly trying to get through the study door. It would have been funny if it weren't for Rabbi Becker's body slumped over his desk. His *kippa* (some of you older people call it *yarmulke*) was askew on what was left of his smashed head. Blood soaked his desk blotter and splattered the pages of the Old Testament on which his head rested.

Leigh noticed the Tree of Life sculpture first. It was still impressive, even with its silver-plated base coated with blood and what looked like the rabbi's dyed black hair and sun-starved white skin. It was the award B'nai Torah planned to give Harry at our fund-raising banquet in a few weeks.

"Don't," I shouted as Leigh stooped to pick up the Tree.

"Why not?" she said in her "I'm-president-of-the-sisterhood" voice.

"Because it may have fingerprints." (I don't watch reruns of *Murder, She Wrote* for nothing.)

"She has a point," Harry said. I'm sure my surprise was plainly written on my face. Harry automatically argues with me no matter what I say, even if I agree with him, which isn't often.

Harry's first claim to fame is his rags-to-riches history. Actually, his rise from poverty more accurately was "tract houses-to-treasury bills." The story is that in the early 1960s Harry got into buying up acres of orchards and farm land northwest of the San Fernando Valley. He covered those acres with ticky-tacky houses, which he sold to eager young families who couldn't afford to live in L.A. And the rest is California real estate history.

His second claim to fame is that for ten consecutive years the board, with Rabbi Becker's encouragement, kept reelecting him president of Heritage Hebrew High, the school financially supported by our *shul's* members. How did he last so long as president of the 300-student religious and secular secondary school when he doesn't even have any kids in the school? Well, if you have to ask, you don't understand *shul* politics.

The fact is, Harry gave big bucks from the first and raises lots more. Why does he do it? My guess is that like most rich men he has to do some atoning for his business "acumen." No doubt he fears that just sitting and praying all day on Yom Kippur isn't going to open the gates of heaven for him. It also didn't hurt that Harry and the rabbi are second cousins.

"Calm down," I said to Hildy and put my arms around her so she could sob on my shoulder. Meanwhile, Sylvia came into the study, saw our late rabbi and after a soft gasp joined Harry and Leigh in their game of frozen statues.

I took charge. "Harry, go use the phone in the business office and call 9-1-1. Sylvia, take Hildy out and get her some water."

My choice of Sylvia over Leigh was easy. Sylvia, a physical education teacher who could deal with a full class of hormone-hyper teens, is far more suited to handling sobbing females than Leigh. In fact, if it weren't for the rabbi's great idea for saving money at the school (decreasing "nonessential" faculty and a mandatory retirement rule), Sylvia would still be one of Heritage's assets.

Leigh, on the other hand, knows how to dress expensively, run a meeting and organize fund-raisers. Dealing with *shul* members, especially those she perceives as less intelligent and less well-off than she, is another matter. Hildy, as the rabbi's secretary, could not avoid the sisterhood president and, as a result, was well acquainted with Leigh's put-downs and temper.

Rabbi Becker, despite his position, also did not pass Leigh's muster. So why did she attend the rabbi's class? It wasn't her thirst for religious learning, believe you me. Simply, she wanted to be sure that the Bible class she had lobbied for succeeded.

She believed (some said justifiably) that the rabbi was over-paid. "He is not doing enough to earn it," she argued at every board meeting, well aware that the rabbi thought he did more than enough. "A rabbi should at least teach a Bible study class," she insisted.

Some *shul* members liked to hint that there was more to Leigh's unhappiness with the rabbi than just his share of the budget, but no one revealed what "more" there was—if anyone even knew.

In the end, Harry got the credit for convincing Rabbi Becker to teach the class. Why would Harry take the trouble? "For the good of the *shul's* members," a generous person might say. The thing is, I've never known Harry or the rabbi to do anything "for the good of the *shul*"—unless it was good for them.

Few people enrolled and the class seemed doomed. "Remember what our sages say," the rabbi pointed out to Leigh and the board, "even if folly succeeds, it's still folly." Knowing Leigh, she would rather try to remedy a situation than admit her idea was folly. Which is why I suspect Leigh decided to attend the class.

***

Detective Melody Fuerza arrived not long after the patrol car officers and the crime-scene unit people. (Thank you, Jessica Fletcher.) Fuerza, a few inches taller than I, had straight hair so black and shiny it looked cobalt blue. She appeared to be in her mid-thirties, but her large dark eyes, the color of aged mahogany, looked ancient.

Fuerza introduced herself, said she would be back to talk to us, then proceeded to enter the "scene of the crime."

Meanwhile, we all waited. The office clock ticked as loudly as a faucet dripping in the middle of the night, and the minute hand jumped every sixty seconds as though it had to catch up. It reminded me of the clocks in the classrooms at Heritage, which were just as cheap and made the same noises. That thought, as usual, led to other annoying thoughts about the way the rabbi and the boards (school and *shul*) penny-pinched. It wasn't just the clocks. Reassured by the rabbi and Harry that the school was doing "a wonderful job of educating its students," and convinced that saving for emergencies was more important, they hesitated to spend money on new textbooks, science lab equipment, computers and other modern educational necessities.

I sighed. It was an old complaint. I brought it up at every meeting, believe you me. I even volunteered my nephew, Ross the CPA, to work out a plan for the school. Some of the money gathering dust could earn money and some could be spent on providing a better education for the children. In all modesty, I think I was getting somewhere. Some board members were listening with one ear, if not yet both.

"What's taking so long?" Leigh asked, breaking into my thoughts. She stood up and began to pace the small space of the *shul* office. "Why can't we go home?"

Although the question was not addressed to me, I felt I should answer. After all, I doubt that any of the study-group members have watched as many TV detective shows or read as many mystery stories as I.

"They'll need to question us about what happened and where we were when it happened," I said.

Leigh's mouth fell open (not very pretty) and her face turned ashen. "Question us? Like for ALIBIS?" She said the last word in shrill capital letters.

"Alibis?" Hildy spoke in a tremulous voice. "The police think one of us killed…?"

I pursed my lips, thinking, then forced myself to stop since it was causing my forehead to wrinkle. ("A pretty face costs effort," Momma used to say.)

"I suppose that's possible," I answered Hildy, and felt a sudden tingle in the vicinity of my spine. This was getting exciting, if you didn't concentrate too much on the rabbi being dead.

Sylvia looked disconcerted. "Are you saying the police think one of us murdered the rabbi?"

"Now hold on, ladies." Harry jumped up and spread his arms wide as though there was a need to keep us from physically attacking each other. He's not the kind of fool who keeps quiet so people will think he's smart.

Hildy, Leigh and I glared at Harry. Still, he went on in a patronizing tone. "No need to get excited. No one's accused anyone.

We need to hear what the police have to say."

I hate to admit it, but he was right.

I was the first to see Fuerza watching us from the doorway and cleared my throat as a warning. Leigh was the first to find her voice.

"I protest your keeping us here so long. It's unconscionable."

"You're...?" Fuerza asked politely, ignoring Leigh's anger.

Leigh pulled herself up to her full five feet two inches. She announced, not gave, her name, sounding as though Fuerza shouldn't have to ask. Me, I wondered what a divorced woman her age, with her face, had waiting at home that she was in such a hurry to get there.

"Ms. Diamond, I'll speak with you first in that office I saw across the hall." Fuerza still spoke politely, but there was authority in her voice that cautioned against arguing. She turned to the rest of us. "I'll want to talk to each of you. I'll have everyone out of here before midnight."

From the look on the faces around me, I could tell no one was sure whether to be happy with Fuerza's promise or angry that they had to stay.

Leigh was gone for only a short time when Fuerza summoned Hildy, then each of us, one at a time, to the office across the hall. I understood when Fuerza got to me why I was saved for last. Like they say, "You save the best for last." Especially when you think it's your best chance to catch a murderer.

***

"Did you speak to Rabbi Becker at any time today?" Fuerza asked after I sat down in the visitor's chair. She was perched on the edge of the desk, relaxed but alert.

I smiled politely. "Hildy probably mentioned I saw the rabbi in his study about an hour before our class."

"For what reason?"

A picture of the skin and hair stuck to what any idiot would guess was the murder weapon flashed in my head, and I considered lying. Then decided that would be dumb for lots of reasons.

"I dropped off the Tree of Life sculpture," I said. "I picked it up this morning from the engravers."

Good, I thought. There's a reason my fingerprints are on it, if the police wonder.

"What did you talk about?"

I breathed a silent thank-you that my answer didn't seem to sound any alarms for Fuerza.

"Nothing. He was sort of…agitated, preoccupied. It looked like he was working on his discussion of this week's portion of the Torah, the Old Testament, for our study group and probably this Sabbath's sermon. This is a major Sabbath, the one before Yom Kippur, our day of atonement."

Fuerza checked her watch. "Getting back to your dropping off the sculpture, is there anything you can remember that Rabbi Becker said or that you said to him?"

I closed my eyes for a moment, happy to imagine Rabbi Becker alive. "He was on the phone when I came in. He was telling someone to 'come before the class.' Then he listened and said, 'Yes, dinner before class. Let yourself in.'"

Fuerza's beautifully arched eyebrows lifted slightly and her eyes opened wider. "Do you know who he was talking to?"

I shook my head. Then I realized why Fuerza was interested in the phone call. "Do you think the person who killed the rabbi was the one on the phone?" The words jumped out of my mouth and into the room before I realized.

She ignored my question. "Do you know who Rabbi Becker was talking to, Ms. Silver?"

"I didn't ask and he didn't tell me." I answered more harshly than I intended, so I added in a softer tone, "Maybe Hildy knows. She keeps his calendar."

"Ms. Newman says she is not aware of any visitors this evening. Except you."

That surprised me. Hildy was like a bouncer at an exclusive bar. No one got past her into the rabbi's study unless she said so. I fleetingly wondered if Hildy was protecting someone.

Maybe herself? I shook off the thought and felt guilty for even thinking it. Everyone knew she and Rabbi Becker had been "keeping company" for a few months. Nothing wrong with that. She's a widow and the rabbi's been divorced for years.

Aloud, I said, "Hildy's very reliable. Maybe whoever it was came while she was out. She takes her dinner break about an hour before class. But she must have told you that."

"And Rabbi Becker?"

"As I said, I saw him in his study when I brought the Tree... Oh."

"Yes?"

"That's what Rabbi Becker must have meant, that he would be alone because Hildy was going to be out of the synagogue for her dinner break... Oh... Whoever it was must have known that Hildy stays on study-group nights and takes a dinner break."

Fuerza's eyebrows lifted again. I hoped she didn't play poker. "What makes you say that?"

I waved my hand as if to wipe away my words, feeling foolish for presuming to tell the police what they must already know.

I shifted in my chair. As my mother used to say, "Guard your tongue. Once said, your words cannot be unsaid."

"Rabbi Becker said 'yes' before he said 'dinner' as though he were confirming what had been said to him, not making arrangements for dinner."

Fuerza gave me a questioning look, and I felt myself turning as red as one of my mother's *kineahora* (anti-evil-eye) ribbons. But I continued: "The person must be someone in our Bible class."

"Whoa," said Fuerza. "How did you come to that conclusion?"

I hesitated. Maybe Fuerza didn't know and it was up to me to help her. I could not protect a murderer, even if it meant losing a *shul* member. Anyway, none of my fellow study-group members were bargains as friends.

I explained. "The rabbi said, 'Let yourself in.' With the doors locked, he had to be talking to someone with a key. Rabbi Becker and Hildy have keys, of course. Leigh, as sisterhood president, has one, and so does Harry, because he's president of Heritage and needs to have access to the synagogue files for fund-raising. Sylvia has one because she takes care of refreshments for the youth group and needs to get in to set up." (I restrained myself from adding, "Elementary, my dear Fuerza.")

"How is it you know who has keys?"

"Hildy told me. I asked her who had keys so I could borrow one. I'm head of the phone committee for the banquet, and we make our calls from the synagogue in the evenings."

Her voice took on a slightly patronizing tone. "So, you know for sure that Ms. Newman locked the doors when she went to dinner, and that it must be someone from the study group because they have keys? How about the maintenance people?" The "gotcha" was in the smile she gave me.

I returned her smile. "The doors are self-locking after evening services, which were over. It's for security, terrorists, you know. And the maintenance people are only here during the day and don't have keys." I hesitated, remembering another key. "Milt Fein, our sexton, is the only other person with a key."

"So it could be this Fein the rabbi was talking to. Is he in your study group?"

I looked down. I really didn't want to embarrass her, even if she was a little rude, but I had no choice. "No, he's not, but I have Milt's key. I borrowed it this morning."

Fuerza cleared her throat. "I see, Ms. Silver. Do you also have a theory as to which study-group member killed Rabbi Becker?"

I shook my head. If she wanted me to do all the work for her, she would have to cooperate. "I need more information." (I wanted to say "clues," but decided she was upset enough.)

Fuerza produced a notepad, studied it for a few moments, then seemed to come to a decision. "Some of this is foreign ground for me. Maybe you can help." I was pleased that she wasn't holding a grudge.

Her eyes were on the wall in back of me, and she looked like she was sorting through her words carefully before she continued. "It appears that Rabbi Becker didn't die right away. We think he tried to tell us something. We found today's desk calendar page clutched in one of his hands. There's a list on it which looks like it was written before his meeting with his murderer. Possibly items he was planning to discuss. He also marked a Bible passage with his other hand."

She paused as though waiting for my reaction. I controlled my excitement at getting this insider information in a real murder investigation by concentrating on the compassion I should have been feeling for poor dead Rabbi Becker.

"'Bea Silver dash nephew' was the first item on the list. Do you know why?"

I was startled. I didn't like being a possible "clue." "The only nephew I ever mentioned to the rabbi was Ross." I told her about my recommendation for a financial plan. "It could be the rabbi was coming to his senses about having someone who knows what he's doing go over the finances."

I heard the usual annoyance I felt about the subject in my voice and stopped talking. I didn't want her to add "anger at the rabbi" to her catalogue of suspicions.

She looked down at her notepad again and read: "Who's 'V. Yayzafe'?"

I started to shake my head. "Do you mean Victor Joseph? He's ninety-four, a retired bank president. He hardly ever comes to synagogue."

She checked her notes again. "Possibly I'm not pronouncing it right. The fingerprint tech is one of your people. Said he hadn't been to temple since he was thirteen, but he remembered enough to read the Hebrew writing from the rabbi's list for me."

"Maybe if I could see it. I used to be a Hebrew studies teacher."

Fuerza hesitated, then took a wrinkled piece of paper enclosed in one of those plastic bags from a folder on the desk and passed it to me. I recognized the rabbi's handwriting, some Hebrew words and some English. When I read what Fuerza must have been referring to, I couldn't keep my laughter in. She stared at me. I pointed to the Hebrew words and explained.

"This isn't someone's name. It's a portion of the Bible with the chapter and verse numbers written in Hebrew letters. '*Vayetze*, chapter twenty-nine, verse twenty-five.'"

I stopped, puzzled. "But that's not this week's portion. That's in Genesis. We studied that last November. It's the story about Jacob being tricked into marrying Leah, instead of Rachel, the woman he loved."

I looked again at the plastic-protected notes and pointed to the paper again. "The next line gives the name of the reading that we were to study tonight and read on the Sabbath. We're almost at the end of *Devarim*, what you call Deuteronomy. It says portion '*Haazinu*, chapter thirty-two, verse five.' It's in the song Moses sings just before he dies and before the children of Israel are to enter the Holy Land."

"And the rest?" she asked.

"The rest are the Hebrew words '*ganavus dot*' and '*Yom Kippur*,' and in English, the letters '*GBC*.'" I noted that each was preceded by a dash, as if they were points the rabbi wanted to make.

"Do you know what 'GBC' means?" Fuerza asked.

I shook my head. "I've seen it before, but I don't remember. Maybe it will come to me after I get some rest."

She missed the hint. "How about the Hebrew?"

With a sigh to get across my weariness, I looked at the calendar page again. "*Ganavus dot* means 'trickery,' but if you translate literally, it means a sort of theft of a person's knowing or knowledge. Yom Kippur, I already mentioned, our day of atonement. It will be in a few days."

Fuerza slipped a Polaroid picture out of her folder, looked at it, then at me. "I have to warn you that you will see some blood in this picture."

She handed the picture to me. It was of part of a Torah page with a man's hand lying awkwardly on it as though pointing. From the small strip of desk blotter in the background and the splattered red dots and dribbles, I had no doubt it was the rabbi's hand, his blood and the Old Testament on which his smashed head had come to rest. A long, uneven blood smear underlining a verse trailed off, ending at the tip of the rabbi's finger. I shuddered. Reality had finally hit me.

"He's pointing to part of the *Shema*, the Hear, O Israel prayer, where it's originally found toward the beginning of Deuteronomy, portion *V'ethannan*."

"Does that mean anything to you?"

"That's one of the prayers of faith often recited by a person dying." I heard the catch in my voice and wondered if she did.

I handed the picture back to her.

"Tell me about the people in your Bible class."

I blew out air between my lips and resigned myself to not going home yet. I felt obligated not to hold back. After all, it was clear to me that the police needed Beatrice Silver to aid them in their investigation. I told Fuerza pretty much what I've already said about the study-group members. Believe you me, I gave her a good picture of the way things in the *shul* were and how I thought they should be. What I couldn't tell her was who killed the rabbi.

***

By the time I got home, I felt like a dishrag rung out too many times in a busy, not too clean coffee shop. Still, I couldn't sleep. Logic told me that whoever killed Rabbi Becker was someone who knew Hildy took a dinner break *and* who had a key. Someone in our class.

How ironic that the Tree of Life was used to take away a life. More significantly, it suggested that the murder was not planned. The sculpture was handy and anyone in the study group could have used it. One unexpected blow to stun the rabbi, then the rest in uncontrolled passion or fear, or both.

But what about the blood? Wouldn't the killer have been splattered with the rabbi's blood?

I plumped my pillow and tried to sleep, but I could not clear away the memory of the blood. Who lived close enough to the *shul* to go home, clean up and still get back before class?

I would have hit my forehead with the palm of my hand if my head didn't ache already. Like a number of Orthodox synagogues, we had a rule that to hold a *shul* position you had to observe at least the basic religious laws. Since traveling by car to attend services on the Sabbath and holidays is a violation of Orthodox religious law, all the "suspects" lived within walking distance of the *shul*. Any one of them had time to let themselves into the deserted *shul*, argue with him, kill him, drive home and come back. But who?

I agreed with Fuerza. The rabbi was trying to tell us.

I got out of bed and pulled my Old Testament off the shelf. I located *Vayetze*, chapter twenty-nine, verse twenty-five: "...it was Leah; and [Jacob] said to Laban 'What hast thou done to me? Did I not serve thee for Rachel? Why hast thou deceived me?'"

Was Leigh an Anglicized version of Leah? Leigh Diamond had a temper and disliked the rabbi. Were the gossips right that her dissatisfaction with the rabbi was about more than how much money he earned? Or was Hildy tricked and deceived in her romance with the rabbi?

Then, what about Jacob working for Laban an additional seven years to earn Rachel? I remembered the rabbi's interpretation when we studied that. "Laban was a thief," the rabbi said. "Through his trickery, he stole seven years of Jacob's life." Did that refer to Sylvia, whose work was "stolen" from her?

I marked the verse with a finger, leafed to *Haazinu*, chapter thirty-two, verse five: "Is corruption God's? No; His children's is the blemish; a generation crooked and perverse." Maybe Harry, who like Laban was a successful businessman, was "crooked and perverse."

I needed more information. I thought again about the wrinkled calendar page.

***

The next morning, I still didn't know who the murderer was.

All I could do was call Fuerza and tell her Rabbi Becker's calendar notes suggested how the police should start their investigation: with my nephew, or at least, with someone looking at the books for the *shul* and the school. She took my advice graciously, and let me know a few days later that, as I expected, the books were far from kosher. Lots of school money was missing.

Too many threads. I needed to weave them together and then, like a tapestry, perhaps a complete picture would emerge. Why had the rabbi used his last moments to find the *Shema*, a prayer even a child can recite by heart? If he lacked the strength to write a message, then was that his message? Like our sages, I decided to look at the written words and search for their hidden meaning.

I opened the Old Testament and located *V'ethannan*. I recalled the rabbi's finger on the page, the blood smear and the point where his finger rested. Verse seven: "...and thou shalt teach them diligently to your children..." As I studied the words, I realized why the rabbi used the phrase *ganavus dot* rather than a simple word for trickery. It was not just trickery, but the theft of knowledge, the literal translation, that Rabbi Becker planned to discuss with his murderer. The verses told me from whom the knowledge was stolen: the children who should be taught diligently, who were blemished by corruption. The rest was easy. The only member of our study group who had access to the funds raised for Heritage and the ability to conceal their theft was Heritage's president and chief fund-raiser, Harry.

The deal Harry's lawyer worked out for manslaughter instead of murder got Harry talking. The surprise was that Rabbi Becker had known all along. Harry was "borrowing" the school's money for years, which, along with his own and the rabbi's money, he used to finance Greenstone-Becker Construction (GBC) projects. Harry, the rabbi and the school made money—until the California real estate market collapsed in the late 1980s. Then, when GBC couldn't sell the commercial properties it had built or pay the mortgages, it borrowed more from the school, until there was nothing left to borrow.

Rabbi Becker, who told Harry he was getting nervous the more it looked like Ross would be going over the books, decided their only hope was to confess to the boards (appropriately) before Yom Kippur. The members would want to avoid public embarrassment, he rationalized. Surely, some of the wealthier board members would cover the losses, and it all could be hushed up. When Harry couldn't argue him out of it, he picked up the Tree and bashed the rabbi with it.

The gossips, by the way, were right about Leigh. She had tried to get Rabbi Becker out of B'nai Torah and her son-in-law, who was looking for a pulpit, in. He found a job in Florida, where Leigh is moving. Hildy, it turns out, had dumped the rabbi for ninety-four-year-old Victor Joseph. Victor isn't demanding and has lots of assets. Sylvia married a retired dentist and moved to Palm Springs.

As for the noise that resulted, the Jewish Education Association instituted an oversight department, which now audits all the religious schools' books in the state once a year. Of course, the IRS was not far behind. Then we really heard the shrieks, believe you me.

JUDITH KLERMAN SMITH was born in Buenos Aires, Argentina. She is a mystery writer and attorney who has published newsletters and legal articles, as well as nonfiction pieces. She has served as coordinator of the annual SinC/LA's "No Crime Unpublished Mystery Writers' Conference" since its inception in 1995.

If Thine Eye Offend Thee

Rosalind Roland

My head must have hit a rock as I rolled down the incline. Blood-thickened hair covered one eye, and I thought I probably ought to get up, but just didn't feel like rushing into anything.

I flexed my ankles a few times, hoping some of the blood not leaking out of me might carry enough oxygen to my brain so I could think again.

It worked.

Bastard, dumbfuck jerks.

I remembered the engine's uphill whine and the stereo bass-line thumping a backbeat. By the time the low-riding black pickup, hitting about forty, had steered into the wrong side of the blind curve ahead of me, I was jogging tight on the edge of the shoulder. I hadn't been worried; I'd been concentrating on cutting a few more seconds off my mile. But the truck didn't pull back into the center; it was aimed at me and the down slope had looked better than the Chevy grille. The last thing I saw was the driver laughing at me, his hairnet low on his forehead.

I could easily have lain there all day watching the eucalyptus leaves flutter above me and feeling the late morning sun on my chest as ants worked their way under my sports bra, if I hadn't begun to feel more anger than pain. He shouldn't have laughed at me.

There was quiet as usual along this stretch of Vista del Sol in Mt. Washington. Houses were scattered through the canyon hills, up slope and down, unlike the rows of small, window-barred homes squeezed along the hot, wide streets below in the flats of northeast L.A. where the road began.

I jumped when I heard shots explode.

I was back on the road, run-limping, pain forgotten, by the time I heard the last two cracks.

A pickup swerved into a Y in the road a hundred feet ahead and briefly braked; no music played. Both rider and driver looked at me, heads turning together. The driver yelled, "*Chinga*, fuck, Hip Hop, which way?"

Then, in a fish-tail skid, they accelerated through the far side of the intersection, taking the alternate road down the hill away from me.

I could hear screams before I made it around the corner. When I had jogged by a few minutes ago, my friends, the Santanas, were setting up a barbecue in the front yard.

Instead of folks hanging up streamers, I saw my daughter, Maggie, on her hands and knees halfway between a tree and the porch steps, vomiting. Lucy Santana's fiancé, Rigo, was lying face-down across the backs of Maggie's legs, not moving, his white T-shirt bloody and pulled halfway out of his pants.

A wide, wet trail ended where Lucy lay on her side. I dragged Maggie from beneath Rigo's legs and ran my fingers over her head, arms and chest. The blood splattered on her was not her own. She was tall for ten, but I carried her up the steps.

Pregnant, seventeen-year-old Lucy had pulled herself up the wooden steps, leaking amniotic fluid and blood. She lay bleeding and quiet, half on the edge of the porch, half on the steps, red lipstick and black eyeliner vivid on her pale face. Rosa, her mother, was curled around her head, rocking.

"It's okay, baby. It's gonna be okay. The ambulance is coming.

Mama's here. Don't leave me, baby. *Holy Mary, Mother of God, pray for us sinners now and at the hour of our death, amen. Hail Mary*—it's okay, okay, sweetie—*be with us now in the hour of our need.*" She chanted, faster than the rhythm of her rocking.

I was an atheist and I still am. Rosa was a Christian and she still is. She prayed, and that day, so did I. I guess our prayers were answered. Sort of. Baby Boy Santana died unborn, but Lucy made it. Sort of. Rigo was dead, but Maggie was alive. Sort of.

***

The day after Lucy came home from the hospital, I watched Rosa push the wheelchair and what was left of her daughter through their front door. I smelled Maggie's vomit again, felt the scars from my fall start to itch.

It got to be a pattern for Rosa and Lucy. And me.

I'd look out my kitchen window down the street where we used to play, and wait for Rosa. I'd watch her carefully roll Lucy into a square of sunlight on the porch. She'd rest there, a bright full skirt hiding the colostomy bag, until her mother wheeled her back in. At first, she sat scrutinizing her mother. Eventually, she just stared at the corner where the pickup had come and gone.

Each day, Rosa went inside after she got Lucy settled, and then returned with an old, galvanized steel washbucket. She'd sit at the top of the stairs with the pail on the step below her and slowly begin washing her way down. It would take all morning to get to the bottom, scrubbing each worn step with hot water and a dish brush, emptying and refilling the bucket after each step.

A ritualistic quality developed, as if she were laving some timeless sacrificial Aztec altar. As if instead of drinking wine that becomes the blood of Christ and the wafer, His flesh, the blood of her child, when finally erased from those steps, might restore the wine of the joy in their youth.

But that wasn't going to happen. Lucy had a dead baby and a dead fiancé; Rosa had a child who'd never walk right again; and I had one who wouldn't talk.

***

I took a leave of absence from my newspaper, and two months after the shooting, I sold my house. I wanted us out of the neighborhood that didn't feel like home, or safe, anymore. I didn't like the idea of a little girl—mine or anyone else's—getting shot by mistake or on purpose. And except for Rosa losing her mind washing away invisible blood, no one seemed to be doing anything about it—at least, not since the initial chaos of the police investigation.

Maggie and I moved into a downtown high-rise, one high enough to see beyond the streets, high enough to see Catalina on a windy day. It had a doorman. It felt secure, concrete-solid, beyond surprise.

After we moved, I spent days with Maggie trying to create new memories, hiking the bridle trails through the Arroyo Seco between L.A. and Pasadena and on up in the Angeles Mountains, hoping she'd find something safe and talk to me again.

***

I didn't want to leave Maggie alone, so I found someone who'd stay with us, since Lucy wasn't baby-sitting anymore. Carla, a student from City College, in exchange for room and board, would be there with Maggie when I wasn't around.

I began driving out of the fifty-story cement canyons, back to the *barrio* flats below Mt. Washington. Telling myself it was therapy, I cruised the Glassell Park, Cypress Park and Highland Park neighborhoods. Conveying little that was park-like these days, they did share the *marcas*, vivid artwork tags, of their own gangs, and parallel moats of taco stands, auto body shops and salvage yards along Verdugo Boulevard or San Fernando Road.

A few *taquerias* had tables and chairs in the parking lot or on the sidewalk. I'd stop at a different one each day, have a Coke, sit for a while and watch the local traffic: uniformed Catholic school kids walking home; low-riders in TransAms and Impalas; seat belt-free, family-crowded cars; beer trucks; and an occasional BMW or Volvo heading toward the hill. I'd read the graffiti on the sides of the buildings, never see Hip Hop, chew on my wounds without distraction and wait for an inner voice or a light from beyond that would lead me out of the past.

Returning after one of these excursions, these failed exorcisms, I took a different route through downtown back to our apartment. I drove past Pershing Square on Fifth to Spring Street. Trapped behind a city bus excreting diesel fumes, I leaned across the passenger seat to double-check the door lock and looked out the window past an old woman sitting on the curb muttering her way through butts in the gutter. Beyond the smudged glass of a pawnshop window leaned a couple of electric guitars next to trays of wedding rings; watches and gold chains rested on a stack of ghetto blasters.

I parked, got out and stood in front of that amalgam of poverty and loss for a long time. Thinking, double-checking my instincts.

I rang the brass button set in the door jamb, and a man in the rear motioned me to slide open the locked iron gate. Another buzzer sounded as he indicated I should push the door.

As I stepped into the smoky dimness of the shop, I shivered. Not from the temperature, but from the chill of emptiness. I was naked. For weeks, the tough fabric of my pacifism had been rotting. I knew that now it was right to be here.

"I want to buy a gun."

***

Rosa had told me a Sergeant Rios was the detective on the case now, a gang specialist. I'd called ahead using a cover about a gang-related story I wanted to do.

Rios was about thirty, lean and tense, with a death's head earring in his left ear. When we shook hands, I saw the shiny-pale scar where a tattoo had been removed between his index finger and thumb. He'd chosen the other side.

I figured he probably remembered my name from the witness reports since I'd talked to the police a couple of times after the shooting. I was counting on his thinking it a little weird if I didn't mention the shooting.

He sat on the window ledge and motioned me to a battered wooden chair in front of a desk. I asked him if he'd heard anything about the guys involved in the Santana shooting, if he knew who the shooter was.

"We're not sure. But probably Hip Hop. We found Mousy, the rider, and he's in juvie for a while, but he's not talking. Looks like Hip Hop disappeared right after the shooting."

"You got any leads? Like where he might be or anything?"

"At first we thought maybe he'd gone down into Mexico. But maybe he's up in Fresno, Bakersfield." He shrugged and stood up to offer me a cigarette. I shook my head.

"Who knows? Says here," he said, holding up a sheet of paper, "Ricardo Mendez. Born in El Sereno, moved over here to Los Avenues *barrio*, grandparents still in Chihuahua, haven't seen him in years. Petty theft, assault, multiple deadly weapons and so on.

"Since the Santana shooting, we been busy. Fifteen shootings, ten knifings. Thirteen homicides in the three months since then. It's summer. A lotta work. Rigo's brother was in a gang. It's not really clear about him.

"I've read the stuff you write. Most of the time, you get your facts straight. You're not as bad as the rest of that scum where you work."

As I agreed with him, I wasn't going to argue about my colleagues, at least two of whom had been on the attack against the LAPD for a couple of years.

"This Hip Hop, he's smart. I gotta tell you, it's not gonna be easy. Some just get away, you know. They stay out of sight, disappear, die. Time passes." He shrugged.

"I'm still looking. We don't have enough men, uh, people. We don't get him for this, though, he'll show up later and we'll get him for something else. Don't worry."

"Yeah? I'm out of that neighborhood now, so I don't worry anymore. I just wondered, you know, how things were going.

"The story I'm working on isn't about him, anyway; it's more like on the girls, the gangbanger *vatas locas,* crazy girls, in *la vida loca,* the crazy life. Like to know why they'd rather fight than be somebody's *ruca.* Is there more power as a fighter than as the girlfriend of a fighter? Or what?"

"A lot of these girls are just plain mean. They like to fight and, yeah, some of it's about power. But something's kinked in them, wound real tight. It's not even like they're crazy; they're just bad," he said, rubbing his scar.

He stood up when I got ready to leave and we shook hands. A nice guy who sounded as though he believed in his work. I almost felt sorry I hadn't been straight with him.

On the way home, I went over what Rios had said. Drive-bys rarely made headlines anymore, and clearly the police didn't think Hip Hop worth more work than any of their other cases. I didn't agree.

Rios had suggested I lose a little of my "social worker" look if I wanted to hang with *las locas,* so I spent some time that afternoon working on my brown hair, getting just the right orangey-platinum streak in front with a deep black fall in the back blow-dried straight. I called my old buddy and manicurist, Harlow Jimenez, and found out she didn't work at the same shop in High-land Park anymore. She'd made it to an old-line beauty parlor in Glendale where they still did back-combing and champagne blond tints. It had been at least a year since I had seen her. I guess we'd both been busy.

When I walked into her shop, I saw only Harlow's location had changed. She still wore four-inch stiletto heels, dyed her hair purple-black and shaved her eyebrows in thin black arcs above white circled eyes. Her nails were so long they curled in on themselves.

"Make 'em like yours," I said.

"You kiddin'? You can't type with these things."

"Yeah, well, okay, not so long, but sexy. Anyway, I don't have a deadline. Mostly, I'm just lookin' around right now."

In the past, we'd gone to a couple of bars together; once her choice, once mine. It wasn't a deep and old friendship as with Rosa, but we could share pain and shame in anonymity.

I watched her build the superstructure at the ends of my nails for a while and then asked her if she'd heard about the shooting in Mt. Washington. I told her I knew the girl who'd been shot.

"Big mistake. Whoever did it," she said, "them *vatos* made a big mistake there. Everybody knows there ain't no homeboys livin' in Mt. Washington. *Estupidos.* You live there, you know that."

"Not anymore. We moved after that boy got killed."

"Don't blame you."

"You ever hear of some dude called Hip Hop?" I said, trying to sound casual and not too interested.

"Nah. Don't think so. Why?"

Here it was. Another lie to a nice person. I was getting good at it.

"I'm doing a story," I said and told her what I'd told Rios, but emphasizing the *ruca* angle.

"Like I said, I don't know. But Tony, he's comin' over tonight and maybe he knows," she said.

About ten o'clock that evening the phone rang. It was Harlow. I could hear salsa rocking in the background, male voices and female laughter. She shouted over the noise: "Hey, Maria—" I became Maria after two tequila shooters. "Get on down here, *chamaca.* Girlfriend, it's time to party."

"Sounds like I'm way too far behind to catch up."

"No way, René." I heard the phone drop and hit the wall. She was laughing and telling somebody to get lost.

"Sorry 'bout that. Look, I'm telling you it's important. There's this chick here. You know, like what you were talking about this afternoon. And you need to get out, anyway."

I didn't need directions. It was the same club we'd been to before. She didn't have to tell me how to dress this time.

I teased and sprayed the top of my hair in a wave so high I was afraid I wouldn't fit in the car. I couldn't bring myself to shave my eyebrows, but my makeup was a tribute to the years I'd spent watching the girls in the flats: black eyeliner, layered eyeshadow and brown lipstick.

Carla and Maggie were curled up reading a book when I asked Carla if I could use her car. I didn't want to take my MGB. Its soft-top was too vulnerable.

"Sure," she said. "You want the junker? I'll get the keys." When she started to stand up, she saw me for the first time. She stopped so abruptly Maggie looked up, too.

"Harlow," Maggie said.

Her psychiatrist had said that when she spoke, it might well be something insignificant, and not to make a big deal out of it.

"Good girl. You got it."

"Dancing."

"Do you mind?"

She shook her head.

I hugged her goodbye until she pulled away.

When I got to the club, a white lunch truck was parked next to the club. Red, white and green twinkle-lights were strung from the hood to the back bumper, *Los Mejores de Juana* written across its side in stylized script. In smaller cursive, Juana advertised: *tacos y tortas, y barios jugos tropicales.*

Competing with those on the truck, much larger red, green and white neon lights ran flashing along the eaves of the club, bringing to life the mural on the side of the building. No socially conscious message here. Just open-mouthed, large-breasted, wasp-waisted women in bikinis dancing on tables with bottles of Corona in their hands. A guy held himself up with one hand braced against the wall while he vomited behind a dumpster. I parked under a light in a red zone across the street.

Inside I found Harlow in a booth. She didn't recognize me at first.

"It's me," I shouted.

"*Orale!* All right," she yelled back. "Hey, you look great."
She patted the seat next to her.

"Tony's here. He's takin' a leak. I gotta talk quick, he's hot
tonight." With my head next to hers, it was easier to hear.

"I asked him about if he knows a *vato* named Hip Hop and he
goes, yeah, he sorta maybe knows him from when Hip Hop was a
kid in the neighborhood. He's a bad dude. Messed up a whole
lotta guys. But the girls are crazy for him, and he's like he can't
get enough pussy. Look at that *puta,* Linda, there in black. Slut.
Look how she's dancing. She used to hang out with him." She
sucked on a lime, hiccupped and pointed out the girl who didn't
look much different than Harlow, or I for that matter.

"I went to school with her big sister. There's a couple others
here Tony says Hip Hop fooled around with, but Linda lasted the
longest."

I asked Harlow to come to the bar with me to get a drink and
maybe introduce us. Another number started and Linda kept dancing. We watched, drinks in hand. I asked her if Tony had said
anything else about Hip Hop.

"Tony, he goes, Hip Hop used to like little *pinche* pussy guns,
but now he wants a big noise, makes him feel big. Shows 'em to
the girls. Tony says he was too pretty for a boy and he tried to act
real macho-like to make up for it. Hip Hop fucked up, though.
Followed some Eighteenth Street *vatos* who was cruisin' on Cypress and lost 'em in the hills. The boy who got shot at that
barbecue, he was the little brother of an Eighteenth Street *vato*,
but that kid was real straight, goin' to college. Usually didn't wear
no colors or nothin'. His brother was real proud of him. Dumb
kid borrowed his brother's jacket that morning. Hip Hop just saw
the colors and that was it."

I asked her if Tony had anything to do with Los Avenues these
days.

"Nah. He's too old now, but he knows what's goin' on. It's
just neighborhoods. First Tony's ol' man and those zoot dudes,
then Tony, and now his dumb nephews."

The music stopped for a minute and Linda walked away from her partner and over to the bar. Harlow motioned for her to join us. She walked over to our table with us and sat down.

"My friend, Maria, here, is a big writer, for one of those *anglo* newspapers. Used to live up jus' off Avenue 43. Went to, you know, St. Bede's."

My right of place established, Linda and I shook hands and I held up the bottle of Cuervo Gold I'd brought back to the table, offering her a drink.

A shot each, camaraderie set, Harlow told her about my story. I asked her if she'd talk to me sometime.

"Hey, no problem. You gonna use my name?"

"Only if you say I can." This thing was taking on a life of its own. I was starting to believe it myself.

She told me we could get together tomorrow. She didn't have to work.

"Hey, here's my ol' man," Harlow said.

Tony came back just then and stood swaying next to us. He said he wasn't too old for anything we might need, or words to that effect. Said he had more *juevos* than that *loco pendejo,* crazy jerk, Hip Hop there, nodding toward the door.

"Nobody ain't seen him around nowhere and now here comes the *lobo* probably looking for some fresh meat," he said, poking his middle finger in and out of the curled fingers of his other hand.

Linda turned so quickly her dark hair, even stiff with spray, swung in front of her face.

"*Cabrón*. Thinks he can just leave me like that," she said standing up. "I gotta tell him to go fuck himself the next time he wants something from me."

Tony laughed and pulled Harlow out of her seat and moved her over to his lap on the other side. I looked through a temporary gap in the dancers and saw Hip Hop strutting up to the bar.

I couldn't see too well because of the couples on the dance floor, but it looked like when Hip Hop got there he turned and grabbed a girl as she walked by. He was holding her still, with the flat of his hand moving in slow circles over her pelvic mound.

Topping off a shot glass from the bottle of Cuervo Gold on the table, I knocked it back. No chaser. Tony's head was lost somewhere in Harlow's chest and they didn't notice when I got up.

On my way to the restroom and a phone across the dance floor, I passed Hip Hop and the girl. She had turned around and was letting him slide his hands up and down her from armpits to hips.

The cop who took my call said Rios wasn't there. I told him who I was and that I'd just seen Hip Hop at Club Tecolote. He said he'd get somebody as soon as possible, but it might be awhile and he wasn't sure there was even a warrant out on the guy. He said there'd been a shooting at Sycamore Grove Park and everybody was over there, adding that I should probably avoid Hip Hop.

Yeah. Right. About then, Hip Hop looked like he was ready to carry that girl out to the back seat of his car and I didn't want him to leave.

Linda moved in front of Hip Hop and the girl. I couldn't hear what they were saying, but I could see her standing there, back arched, one hand on a cocked hip and the other shaking a finger at him.

I walked over to the bar and stood next to her, watching the back of his head and her face in the mirror. I could hear his laughter, her angry voice and the other girl's voice. There was a great deal of *puta*, bitch, etc., going back and forth. He seemed to be enjoying it until Linda told him to shut up and called him a few names.

He shook his head and said, "Just get outta here, okay. Leave me alone," and turned around to the bar.

I moved sideways at the same time and he rubbed his arm across my chest. I gasped and crossed my arms in front of me. He didn't notice my face. Instead, he looked at my breasts, which were bulging above the neckline on my dress. I smiled up at him to let him know I knew it was an accident.

"Wouldn't wanna hurt nothin' lookin' so good."

"Buy me a drink and prove it," I said.

He handed me a beer and said, "Dance," putting his arm around my waist and moving me to the center of the swaying couples.

"What about your friends?" I said and nodded toward the women who had moved away together.

"Don' worry 'bout them, they're nobody."

Out on the floor, he managed to hold a cigarette and beer in one hand and squeeze my butt hard enough to hurt with the other.

"I ain't seen you around here before an' I woulda remembered."

I didn't say much, just moved in closer. He jerked back when I touched the scar under the spider-in-a-web tattoo on the side of his neck.

He smelled like fresh sweat, Aqua Velva and weed. Another scar broke the black line of his eyebrows; he didn't look pretty anymore, but I didn't care what he looked or smelled like. I just wanted to keep him there.

"You dance good," he said later. "You wanna go some other place I know?" I told him I wanted to stay with my girlfriend and pointed over to where Harlow and Tony were, but they had gone.

"Looks like she left you. I saw her all over that ol' *veterano*."

I looked at my watch and saw it had now been over an hour since I called. The cops should have been here by now.

"Sure, why not, but I'll take my own car." I not only felt safer driving myself, I didn't want to leave it where it was. I told him to meet me by my car; I needed the bathroom.

He didn't frighten me. Much. He'd had a lot to drink and even if I felt the tequila and beer, I hoped I could outrun him. I was a toy, not a threat.

I watched him leave and he didn't say goodbye to anyone. I dialed the station three times and kept getting a busy signal. I decided to try again when we got to the next place.

No one saw us leave.

I followed him as he turned off Cypress away from the business section. Streetlights were broken and blackness stretched the blocks. The wheel spun free through my cold, sweaty hands on the last turn, but I wasn't about to go back.

It wasn't a club we went to; it was an apartment building. A two-story frame building built in the twenties, it had torn window screens behind bars on the ground floor. Graffiti covered the retaining wall in front, the cracked sidewalk and the porch. There was a vacant lot on one side and an abandoned house on the other.

He pulled into a driveway and I parked in the shadow underneath an old black walnut tree. The streetlight at the curb was broken and there was no moon. He walked over to my side of the car, slicking his hair back, flipping his long queue-like braid over his shoulder.

"This is it, baby. Les' go."

"This your place?"

"One of my homey's. What's the difference?"

Maybe I could get him to another club or restaurant later, someplace with a phone. He wasn't going anywhere now.

I left the key in the ignition and the gearshift in first, ready to roll. This was not a car anybody would want or remember. Wires stuck out where the radio had once been, the windshield was cracked, and it had no back seat.

When I slid out he pushed me against the car and tried to kiss me. My purse was in the way and he yanked it off my shoulder.

"Whatcha got in there?" he said shaking it by the strap.

I grabbed him around the neck and pulled his head down, my mouth almost on his, and whispered, "Ey, *hombre*, it's not what's in there you want."

"You think you're one tough bitch," he said, pushing me back against the door until it hurt, holding the purse away from him with a straight arm.

"Not tough, just gettin' very hot, *muy calentura*." His left knee slipped in between my legs.

"I only got girl stuff in there," I said reaching for my bag. "Now, you gonna go dancing with me, or you wanna stay here and act bad?"

"This ain't no act, *culo,* cunt, and I can tell you like it."

"I don't like it when you call me names," I said and dug my nails into his bare arm. He dropped the purse on the ground by my feet and squeezed my cheeks together with his hand under my chin pushing my lips out. He kissed me like that, my teeth cutting the insides of my mouth. I tasted my own blood and remembered.

I relaxed and slid down to sit-ride his knee. There was a party going on somewhere at the far end of the block and I could hear the bass-line pumping in the distance. Like every weekend, fireworks cracked the night.

"You don't get no bed, *puta*, you gonna get it right here," he said, dropping to his knees in front of me, one hand pulling my dress down below my breast and the other reaching under my skirt. My ears were ringing and my hands were shaking on his shoulders. I felt his breath on my bare skin, and I tried to loosen my jaws, relax my stomach. I let myself slide farther down the side of the car.

"I like your perfume. You got anymore in there?" he said, pointing at my purse.

I nodded.

"Put some down there."

He was on his knees in between my legs and he scooted my purse over to me. With one hand I flipped back the flap and groped around, scrabbling through brushes, papers, watching him unzip himself, feeling him pull my skirt up and tear away my panties. I licked my lips and tasted blood again. His erection poked through the open fly as his pants slipped off his hips.

"Kiss me there if you're so bad," I said.

"Fuck you. I don't go down on nobody."

"Do it or you don't get anything." I pulled out my perfume and told him to open it for me. I spilled it on my belly and rubbed it between my legs.

"Now do it."

He grabbed my thighs and lifted them up, stretching his body flat on the ground, and put his head where I'd asked. I held myself still and laid my legs over his shoulders, stroking his back with my heel. When he started moaning, I said, "Look at me."

He raised his eyes and I fired straight into his left pupil.

His head rocked back and I rolled sideways and up on my knees. I felt nothing. He twitched a few times and I could tell he'd fouled the ground beneath him.

I pulled him over and pressed my fingers to his wrist, then his throat. He had no pulse.

I held the muzzle to his right eye and fired again.

The party up the street was louder than ever. No cars had driven by. No lights came on. I took a penlight out of my bag and checked the rough scrub grass where we'd been lying. Nothing had spilled out of my purse. I got in the car and backed out without turning on my lights.

The next day, Sergeant Rios called and said he was sorry he'd missed me at the club. By the time they got there, I was gone, but they'd found Hip Hop, anyway. Looked like the Eighteenth Street *vatos* found him first, though, and left a *marca* of sorts. Both eyes shot out. No witnesses. Looked like that was it. Saved the taxpayers a lot of money, too.

"If thine eye offend thee, shoot it out?" he said and laughed.

I thanked him and went into my bathroom, cut up my somewhat stained dress and piece by piece flushed it down the toilet. I washed out the black rinse, dyed the platinum back to brown and cut my nails.

ROSALIND ROLAND began writing tales of pioneer days when she was nine, while she waited to move to the western frontier. When she learned that California, her home state, was the Far West, she switched to writing mysteries. She has since written for *L.A. Weekly* and has had fiction published in *West/Word*.